"Can I help it if I'm picky?" Laine asked

"Besides," she continued, "names are a very important factor in other people's perception of you."

"What about Colin?" Murphy asked with idle curiosity. "What does my name mean?"

She eyed him pointedly. "Colin means young, strong and virile. Which only goes to show that a name isn't always reliable."

He smiled and took a step toward her, forcing her to back up until she was pressed against the wall. "That sounds like a dare to me, Sunshine. Are you asking me to prove something?" His voice sounded soft. Seductive.

"Come on, Murphy," she challenged. "You're not cut out to play the sexually menacing aggressor."

He drew her slowly toward him, so that they were almost touching. "Maybe you're not as perceptive as you think," he said, looking straight into her eyes.

Laine had no time to wonder what he meant. His mouth took hers as he fitted their bodies in close, erotic alignment....

Kate Jenkins has done it again! After being nominated for an RWA Golden Medallion for her first Harlequin Temptation, *On the Wild Side*, she has come up with another equally warm, upbeat romance with fun-loving characters. *Suddenly, Sunshine* is the type of romance Kate loves to read . . . and to write.

Kate says it was while working in such varied fields as teaching, counseling and banking that she collected a wealth of different characters and stories—a good reason to try her hand at romance writing.

Kate and her husband live in Houston, where they run their own business.

Books by Kate Jenkins
HARLEQUIN TEMPTATION
182–ON THE WILD SIDE

Suddenly, Sunshine

KATE JENKINS

Harlequin Books

TORONTO • NEW YORK • LONDON
AMSTERDAM • PARIS • SYDNEY • HAMBURG
STOCKHOLM • ATHENS • TOKYO • MILAN

Published November 1988

ISBN 0-373-25327-3

1

LAINE RANDOLPH COUNTED only three women in the assembled group of twenty, and every man—save one—looked promising.

She paused in the doorway, silently applauding her friend Claire's suggestion that Laine sign up for a goal-setting seminar at this North Carolina mountain retreat. When she'd phoned about the first available session, it was already full. Laine had used her negotiating ability and persuaded the coordinator to admit one more person.

She hadn't come here because she needed to learn about goal setting. Laine had set her course months ago. But her thirtieth birthday, the self-imposed deadline for reaching that goal, was only a few weeks away. She didn't have any time to waste.

Anticipation made her smile and added sparkle to her intensely blue eyes. The next five days were going to be very challenging, she thought, finger combing her sun-streaked light brown hair as she breezed dramatically into the room.

"I hope I haven't kept you waiting," she apologized breathlessly, alighting in the empty chair next to a slouching man who appeared to be asleep. "I took a wrong turn several roads back and ran into the most fascinating character." She rummaged through the depths of an enormous tote. "I couldn't offend him by rushing off, especially after he offered to teach me how to whittle."

Laine displayed a grossly misshapen wooden piglet, complete with curly tail. "Not bad for a beginner, huh? Of course Boggy—that's the old guy with no teeth and a face full of whiskers—assures me that I'll get much better if I practice every day." She appraised the carving from all angles, frowning slightly before directing another sunny smile toward her audience. "What do you think?"

Impeccably suited or elegantly casual, they all regarded her with equal amounts of curiosity and disbelief. But no one spoke. Laine figured some insidious additive in their collective hair sprays had rendered them mute.

She shrugged and tucked the unappreciated pig into a side pocket of the tote, muttering under her breath, "Guess they aren't interested in art."

"Philistines," a gruff voice drawled so softly that she almost missed it.

Laine chuckled as she flicked a quick glance at the man next to her. How incongruous that someone dressed in well-worn denim, a lurid floral print shirt and abused yellow running shoes would have the audacity to comment on the fashion plates' lack of culture.

Suppressing a giggle, she eyed the splash of pink and green orchids. "Obviously you're far more discerning."

"Taste always shows."

His voice, along with the wry wit, struck a familiar chord, and Laine swiveled, studying the tanned, craggy profile. She recognized him from a recent interview on an Atlanta television news program. She'd also read several magazine features that detailed his work. He'd impressed her as talented, articulate and individualistic, with just enough self-deprecating humor to temper a healthy self-confidence. He didn't, however, seem like the type who'd attend a goal-setting seminar.

"Colin Murphy! Imagine running into you here."

"Mmph," he grunted, still slumping in his seat, arms crossed, chin resting on his chest, eyes unreadable behind tinted glasses. "You have me at a disadvantage, Ms—?"

"Of course I do," she agreed cheerfully, passing up the opportunity to supply her name. "I have a feeling that doesn't happen often. How do you like it?"

His spine lazily conformed to the padded cushion, but one foot pumped up and down in a frenetic rhythm. "Probably not as much as you like putting men in their place."

He was uncomfortably close to the truth, but she was unusually adept at changing the subject. With long-practiced ease, she focused on what most men like best to talk about—themselves and their work.

During the past decade, Colin Murphy had been building an enviable reputation as an architect. His designs were diverse—from soaring glass-sheathed towers of pristine simplicity to an oil sheikh's palace that Murphy had described as being of the neobombastic school. But when asked by the interviewer to name his single most rewarding achievement, Murphy had replied dryly, "Keeping the critics from categorizing me." Laine had liked that.

"Do you really not mind that people in Atlanta are calling your new building an overblown Band-Aid box?" she inquired.

A barely discernible dip of his head was the only sign that she might have struck a nerve. "It's always rewarding to run into people who appreciate my work."

Laine was glad that he sounded more amused than insulted. Strangers often misinterpreted her bluntness. She grinned playfully. "I happen to like the building. I only asked if criticism bothers you."

His foot stilled for a few seconds, then resumed its steady beat. "I guess most people want a certain amount of approval." He tugged a lock of hair that curled onto his collar and made a vague gesture with his other hand. "But it's not necessary for everyone to like my buildings. What's important is that they notice them, think about them. Remember them. Beyond that, they're entitled to their opinion." He paused, smiling slyly. "It's not my fault if they can't recognize brilliance."

Laine's brain was tripping over a hundred questions she wanted to ask him. She had a weakness for eccentricity and creativity. Combined, the traits were even more enticing. She gave herself a mental slap. She was here to check out the available males, not for intellectual stimulation. Laine's internal debate halted when their seminar leader arrived and promptly launched into the business at hand. Amanda Hunt was young, attractive and obviously skilled at grabbing an audience's attention.

"The first step to reaching a goal is to articulate it. So before we get caught up in names, companies or titles, I want each of you to stand up before the group and state one of your goals. Who wants to volunteer?"

The leader's eyes rested briefly on her, but Laine didn't take the cue. She wanted to be last. Though it wasn't her intention to disrupt the program, there was no denying that her stated goal would probably cause a furor. Accustomed to speaking her mind, Laine wasn't going to sugarcoat her true purpose for these strangers.

The man on the other side of Laine—the one who made sure his Rolex watch was always visible—spoke up. From there they progressed around the circle.

Laine listened as each one of the almost exhaustingly aggressive achievers announced his or her plan to become either a corporate president, the top-producing salesperson, the owner of a company, a majority stockholder, a millionaire. They were so predictable in their pursuit of status and money that eventually Laine made a game of guessing all the participants' goals before they stated them.

Murphy stage-whispered in her ear, "All this rampant success makes me nervous. They have to be doing something dishonest."

Laine smiled, not surprised by his opinion. She couldn't wait for his turn. Something told her that his goal might be as incomprehensible to this crowd as her own.

When the others had finished, Murphy made an exaggerated production of getting to his feet, as if he resented the effort. He planted one foot assertively on the rung of his chair and hooked both thumbs into his belt loops, long fingers resting lightly against the front of his jeans. With his hips thrust forward slightly, his stance hinted defiance, and something else Laine didn't want to examine too closely. She moistened her lips and leaned forward, feeling strangely restless.

"I want to make *Playgirl*'s list of the ten sexiest men in America."

Dumbstruck, Laine witnessed a typical example of group dynamics in action. Most of the people started to snicker, thought better of it, and covered up their blunder by sitting even straighter.

How was it possible, she wondered, that Murphy, who looked neither impressive nor menacing, could make a room full of hard chargers squirm in their seats because they'd dared to laugh at him? He wasn't tall; probably an inch, maybe two, under six feet. His rangy build was unremarkable; he posed no physical threat. But a kind of quiet invincibility radiated from him, as though he were a law unto himself, unconcerned about what anyone else thought of him.

There was something incredibly irresistible about a man so at ease with himself.

Laine had learned to never underestimate people who possessed that intangible, yet unmistakable quality. They were sure of what they wanted, and certain of how to get it. His goal was so blatantly tongue-in-cheek that it never occurred to her to take it seriously. And yet, something about the man himself precluded the obvious reaction. She hadn't laughed either.

As she took the floor to drop her little bombshell, Laine tried to convince herself that she didn't find Murphy and his attitude enormously appealing. He was hardly her ideal candidate for a husband. But it was impossible to deny that not one of the other men sparked her interest half as much as the patently unsuitable Colin Murphy. *Forget it*, she ordered. *Concentrate on why you're here.*

With that in mind, she stepped closer to the center of the semicircle to be sure she had everyone's attention. She made eye contact. That showed sincerity. She gave them her best toothpaste-ad smile, an action that needed no justification because it came naturally, without design. Then she said, in a clear, confident voice, "I want to get married."

The only sound in the room was a muffled snort.

LAINE WAITED TO APPROACH the leader until everyone else had straggled out of the meeting room. Since they were about the same height, five foot five, Laine could look directly into Amanda Hunt's blue-gray eyes. "I hope you don't think I was ridiculing the purpose of this seminar when I said I want to get married. I meant it. Finding a husband has been my goal for the past year." With a resigned sigh, she shouldered her heavy tote. "Unfortunately, my efforts have met with a stunning lack of success."

Amanda chuckled and tucked a wisp of short chestnut hair behind her ear, a habit Laine had observed more than once during the past hour. "Actually your declaration was rather refreshing. I've been holding these seminars for several years, but you're the first person who's ever admitted that her aim was marriage. A lot of women think getting married indicates that they're not serious about their careers."

"Who cares about that?" Laine scoffed. "I don't need to prove anything. I've been on my own long enough to know I can take care of myself. I own half of a company that makes more money than I need to satisfy me. But it's not enough. Something is missing."

"I understand how you feel," Amanda said, tracing her gleaming, wide gold wedding band. "Don't ever apologize for your goals, whatever they are. If you set them, they're important to you, which is all that matters."

Watching Amanda gather her material from a table, Laine felt a kinship with the other woman, though they had just met. The two of them drifted out of the room, exchanging small talk as they strolled toward the rustic lodge's reception area.

"Just between us," Amanda confided, "I think you and Colin Murphy are going to make this one of the most unusual sessions I've ever conducted. Even though Mr. Murphy's motivation for being here is quite different from anyone else's. Including yours," she added with a lift of one brow. They stopped at the foot of a stairway that led to the second-floor guest rooms.

"He didn't come to learn about goal setting?"

"No, that's not why he's here. Anything beyond that you'll have to find out for yourself." Amanda smiled as she gazed out an oversize window at the tennis courts nestled amid dense trees. "I think it *is* safe to assume that he has no real desire to make anyone's 'ten sexiest' list."

A little ripple of sensation settled in Laine's stomach. Why did the least likely men sometimes have the most devastating effect? She cleared her throat and asked, "Don't you think that Murphy is being condescending toward your objectives and methods?"

"Who knows," Amanda said, unruffled. "I am convinced that his goal was probably thrown out for shock value, to see what kind of response it would draw. I imagine he likes putting people on."

The same thought had occurred to Laine. It had been clear to her that Murphy was faintly, maybe flagrantly, contemptuous of those who were so driven to succeed. But with his *Playgirl* announcement he'd effectively changed the tenor of the whole session.

"That was something to see, wasn't it? Almost like a showdown. And yet, nothing really happened. Extraordinary," Laine marveled. She'd thought her goal would cause a sensation, but Murphy had almost upstaged her.

"As I said, neither of you fits the profile of the average seminar participant."

"I doubt if Murphy fits any profile known to man," Laine ventured, annoyed that she found his singularity so damned intriguing.

"Maybe that's what makes him so damned intriguing," Amanda echoed in an eerie counterpart to Laine's thoughts.

WHY IS SHE SO DAMNED intriguing? Colin Murphy asked himself, squinting through the branches of a potted plant to unashamedly spy on Elaine Randolph. He'd figured that reclusive thirty-six-year-old cynics had some sort of immunity to bewitching women.

But from the moment she'd made her grand entrance earlier that afternoon, everything about this woman had demanded his attention. She fascinated him. So much so that he could almost forgive Andy for this latest in a long line of outrageous birthday gifts. Murphy had cursed his best friend for sentencing him to five days in the North Carolina mountains with a bunch of tiresome, dynamic goal setters. Andy knew Murphy wasn't a mountain person, that he got both peace of mind and inspiration from the ocean. He knew, too, how much Murphy disliked being around strangers, especially aggressive ones. He'd warned Andy that he would pay dearly for this fiasco.

Andy had laughed and told him to make the best of it, that maybe some delightful surprises awaited Murphy. He hadn't bought it at the time, but Elaine Randolph had given him a new perspective.

Andy would be guffawing if he knew that Murphy had forgotten his bias against meaningless socializing, had gotten semi-dressed up and had come to this get-acquainted party. He'd even sneaked in early so he could steal a peek at the female name tags. By discreetly rearranging them, he'd been able to find out her name when she'd claimed hers. Ironically, he admitted that he was acting like one of those weirdos who populate bad detective novels. Still, he didn't take his eyes off Elaine Randolph.

She was wearing something vibrantly red and clingy, yet, on her the overall effect was casual, comfortable. It sounded trite, but she looked like the all-American, girl-next-door type. Fresh and pretty, but not in an exotic or contrived way.

Was *tawny* the word for her mixture of blond and light brown hair? Whatever the color, he liked the loose curls that brushed her shoulders and swayed as she moved. You could take her out in a convertible knowing she wouldn't be glaring daggers at you and fussing about her hairdo.

Murphy wasn't close enough now to see, but he'd memorized several details when she'd sat next to him in the afternoon. Other than a little mascara on her eyelashes and a touch of something glossy on her lips, her beauty was natural, and all the more appealing because of it.

As she greeted another besotted Romeo, Murphy wondered with a shade of irritability if she'd ever felt ill at ease with strangers. Ever watched the action from the sidelines. Probably not. If this crew was any example, Elaine Randolph charmed everyone she met, male or female.

Like a hummingbird, she hovered, sampling briefly, then darting to the next flower. No, he decided with a frown. Her movements were spirited, but not frenzied. Maybe she was more like a brilliant butterfly, gracefully fluttering about, looking for a place to settle. Murphy's frown deepened. That wasn't quite accurate, either.

His creative ability was failing him in this, too. He wasn't having any better luck thinking of the correct analogy for Elaine Randolph than he'd had in coming up with a unique design for that government complex in Wisconsin.

Suddenly, like an inspiration, it came to him fully developed. She was the single ray of sunshine that somehow penetrates a gloomy day, drawing all eyes to its radiance. Creating happiness with its presence. A disgusted snarl vibrated in his throat. Sunshine indeed! He was pretty far gone when he resorted to such sappy, simplistic descriptions of a woman.

But he couldn't chase away the image. In his mind, Elaine Randolph and sunshine were one and the same.

He watched her return a sparkling smile to the good-looking man whose intentions, Murphy was sure, were less than honorable. Couldn't she tell that guy was as phony as a three-dollar bill? He supposed this little mating ritual was inevitable, given her declaration that she wanted to get married. But he'd stake a hefty fee that not one of these posturing males was shopping for a wife.

Being a man, he had a pretty good idea of what was on their minds.

"Damn," he swore softly. He couldn't hear what she'd said that had completely shocked her latest victim, then made him shrug his shoulders good-naturedly and melt back into the crowd of would-be suitors.

He'd been watching her shuffle and deal the available men for nearly an hour, and his temper was growing more uncertain by the minute.

Elaine—she didn't look like his concept of an Elaine—smiled with annoying frequency, as though everything and everyone she encountered pleased her. Murphy felt a perverse need to make her mad, to see the smile vanish. At least that would distinguish him from the rest of the pack. He untangled himself from his protective cover and crept up behind her.

"Saving yourself for marriage, Miss Sunshine?"

"You can bet I'm saving a thing or two."

Her tone sounded teasing, but she didn't turn around so he couldn't be sure. He stepped forward and half turned to face her.

"Shame on you for lurking in the shrubbery, Murphy," she scolded, making him suspect that she'd known he was there all along. "Why didn't you come out and join the fun?"

"I hate cocktail parties," he said grumpily, as if that were a reasonable explanation for sneaking around like a second-rate gumshoe. "Elaine," he added, his gaze dropping to linger on the name tag pinned just above her breast.

"Laine," she corrected after a moment's hesitation, drawing his gaze upward with the soft lilt of her voice. "*Everyone* hates cocktail parties." She pointed to the crowded, noisy room. "Which, I suppose, is why so many people go to them."

She still wore the same sparkling smile, and he could almost forget his need to anger her. Murphy liked having that smile directed at him. But it wasn't reserved exclusively for him, he reminded himself. She blessed everyone equally. "What was wrong with that last candidate? He looked like the best of the lot."

Laine rolled her eyes heavenward. "He told me he's a bodybuilder. Actually, he said it in sort of a boastful way, as if he thought it was something to be proud of."

"It's not?" He thought women liked that type of man, the more brawn the better.

"Be serious, Murphy. Don't you know how obscene those characters look without their clothes?" She wrinkled her nose. "All those palpitating pectorals and quivering quadriceps remind me of a genetic experiment gone haywire."

"You're not impressed by mutant muscles?"

"Nope. I don't need to be overwhelmed."

Murphy realized she was looking at him with an intensity that matched his own. At that moment, he had a crazy urge to do just that. Overwhelm her. Beginning with... "Uh, how about that one?" he forced himself to ask, gesturing toward another guest.

"He's a Scorpio. Any sane woman knows they're overloaded with passion. I sure don't need that."

Murphy choked back a coughing fit. "Where do you come up with all these weird notions?"

Laine laughed at the question because she'd heard it often before. "I'm addicted to trivia and afflicted with almost total recall. I can entertain or bore people with helpful information for hours."

"I can see all that will be invaluable in your search for a husband. What's *his* problem?" Murphy asked, inclining his head toward the stiff-spined man ordering a drink at the bar.

"He recently retired from the military to start a consulting business. I know the type. He'd probably expect me to salute and call him *sir*." Eyes alight with mischief, she cupped her hand around her mouth and confided solemnly, "And there'd be those daily inspections to make sure the bed-sheet corners were mitered. I don't know about you, but I like to wallow around in my sheets, not bounce quarters on them."

Murphy laughed at her not-so-elegant description. But the idea of doing anything in Laine Randolph's sheets made him shift restlessly. He hadn't even made up his mind whether she was appallingly flaky or delightfully candid, but his body was way ahead of him, insisting that it didn't matter.

"Easy for you to laugh. Your father probably wasn't a colonel."

"No," he admitted. "Is yours?"

"Worse, I'm afraid. He just kept polishing his bird until finally that little sucker turned into a star." She saw that he wasn't following her drift. "He's a general now. Smokin' Joe Randolph. A classic fast burner, as they're called in the Air Force." She stood erect and snapped her heels together. "Of course they have other names for him, but they might shock an innocent such as yourself."

"Sunshine, they haven't invented anything that could shock me."

"Oh, dear. I guess you must be from California." She sighed heavily. "Do you people get issued a permit to be jaded and cynical along with your driver's license?"

Somehow she always said what he least expected. Murphy didn't correct her misconception about where he lived, but she had a point about the other. He'd played at being a cynic for so long that he'd slipped into the role without thinking. Aside from those few people closest to him, everyone accepted it as natural. The glint in Laine Randolph's eyes gave him the uncomfortable feeling that she'd seen through the ruse and was taunting him about it. Murphy wasn't sure he liked that.

"What about your act—" he countered, "—your bid for marriage?" His gaze skimmed up and down her figure, as if he were evaluating it with cool disinterest, a feat that was hard to accomplish when his blood was heating rapidly. "You're a good-looking woman, Laine Randolph. You don't need theatrics to get a man's attention. And the odds here are definitely in your favor." Although there were a few other women at the party, they were still a minority.

"I was serious," she said slightly on the defensive. "Last year I set a goal to be married by my thirtieth birthday. I've only got a few weeks left. I can't afford to be subtle."

Murphy wondered if that was what she really wanted, or why she'd approach her goal in such a capricious manner. But because he needed to get a fix on her, he probed further. "If you're that desperate, why did you dispense with most of the prospects in such a hurry?" His sweeping gesture encompassed the rejects.

"Can I help it if I'm picky? I plan to keep the same husband for the next fifty years or so. I can't settle for just any man merely because he's willing."

"I assume all the discards had fatal flaws. That one, for instance." He singled out a man at the buffet table who looked uncannily like television's latest heart-throb.

"Wears a pinky ring," she said, dismissing him as if his choice of jewelry constituted an unforgivable transgression. "And the guy next to him . . . too prissy. He called me 'my dear'. I couldn't tolerate that insipid endearment for the rest of my life."

"Of course not," Murphy sympathized sardoni-cally, following her to the bar. "And his problem?" he questioned, directing his gaze across the room to the slick, grinning predator who seemed to be biding his time while plotting another advance.

"His name is Dennis," Laine said, giving the bar-tender one of her heart-stopping smiles.

"Dennis," Murphy repeated, feeling as though he'd landed in the middle of a fractured fairy tale. "I doubt that I'll understand, but what's wrong with the name Dennis?"

"It means lover of fine wines," she explained pa-tiently, making him feel like a slow learner. "He might turn into an alcoholic. You can't take chances on a thing like that."

"I don't believe this!" he almost shouted, not stop-ping to consider that her loony ideas didn't concern him. "It's ludicrous to rule out someone for such a crazy reason."

"I like to take everything into account," she said, unperturbed. "Names are very important in how people perceive themselves and others." Laine looked away momentarily to tell the young man behind the bar, "I'll have a glass of that white zinfandel." After watching it being poured, she tilted the stem toward Murphy. "How about you?"

"I don't like wine. I don't trust people who drink it."

Laine halted the glass halfway to her mouth, then very deliberately set it back on the bar. The muted thunk of glass against wood sounded nearly as articulate as a verbal challenge.

"I don't trust anyone whose eyes I can't see."

As quickly and decisively as she had relinquished her wine, he whipped off his tortoiseshell-framed aviator glasses. *Oh, Lord,* Laine rued silently, staring, sinking into Colin Murphy's green-flecked golden eyes. *Why didn't I keep my mouth shut?*

Eyes like his were lethal. They had been persuading women—probably ever since the Stone Age—to succumb to all manner of foolish, impetuous acts. They saw too much, but revealed only enough to say, *You're in trouble now.* Murphy's eyes belonged in someone's bedroom.

Shaken, Laine grabbed for the abandoned wine and took a generous gulp to restore her control. "Put your glasses back on. You must need them to see." She felt smug at how unaffected her voice sounded. He'd never guess that her pulse had gone berserk. On second thought, if his lopsided grin was any indication, maybe he *had* guessed. She downed another swallow.

He followed her order, then aimed one finger at a bottle of imported beer. The bartender quickly uncapped it and handed it to Murphy. He took it, but didn't drink. "What about Colin?" he asked with idle curiosity. "What does my name mean?"

She eyed him pointedly, debating the merits of answering truthfully. The awareness of having just survived a narrow escape still hummed inside her. But she could handle that—and Murphy, Laine told herself with hastily fabricated optimism. "Colin means young, strong and virile. Which only goes to show that these factors aren't always reliable."

He smiled and took a step toward her, forcing her to back up until she was pressed against a wall. "That sounds like a dare to me, Sunshine. Are you asking me to prove something?"

Laine drained the contents of her glass. Her throat stayed dry. She regretted starting this conversation. She'd have been safer latching on to that self-proclaimed millionaire who evidently thought an excessive dose of cologne substituted for mouthwash. "You're not so young," she asserted, chagrined that she'd apparently made an unconscious decision to continue with this line. She looked thirstily at the bottle of wine on the bar, and calculated her chances of escaping.

"Maybe not. But of course, age is relative." He appeared to be reading the label on his bottle, but Laine wasn't fooled by the delaying tactic. "What's the verdict on my strength?"

"You're no heavyweight," she told him with a willful lift of her chin. As if that mattered. Men like Murphy didn't need brute strength. They had other, more potent weapons.

He set his beer down on a convenient table and gently plucked the wineglass from her hand to place it beside the green bottle. "You said it yourself. You don't like to be overwhelmed." As if defying his own words, Murphy grasped her upper arm and before Laine knew it, he'd whisked her away from the crowd and into a shadowy alcove.

Suddenly they were alone. Murphy removed the glasses, tucking them in his pocket. In the heat of his gaze, Laine's goal receded, as distant as the party sounds.

"Let's see," he said, stroking his chin, "what was that third—? Ah yes. Now I remember. Since you've shot me down on the other two, I guess I'll have to exert a little extra effort to prove my virility. Is that what you want?"

"Come on, Murphy. If you think that's what I want, you're far less perceptive than I'd have imagined. You're really not cut out to play the sexually menacing aggressor." Laine hoped he was more convinced by her words than she was.

His voice sounded soft and raspy. Seductive. It sent chills cascading over her. Not the creepy kind. The delicious kind, like the ones she got from listening to a virtuoso violinist or the *Hallelujah Chorus*. "You don't think so? Then maybe *you're* not as perceptive as you thought."

His hands rested lightly on her shoulders and Laine felt an unnatural heat penetrating through the thin barrier of silk. "Murphy, please." It was hard to sound decisive. She wasn't even sure what she was asking of him.

"The way I figure it, I ought to be the authority on how to please you. You've spent the past half hour telling me all the things you didn't like about those men you cast off. I could give them lessons."

His fingers flexed, drawing her toward him so that they were almost touching. Laine had to tip her head back to see his face. His eyes were again concealed by the tinted glasses, except that now she knew how dangerous they could be.

His voice turned low and beguiling. "All those other guys wanted to impress you and failed. But if I was making a play for you myself, I wouldn't think about anything except Murphy's law."

"You mean, that if anything can go wrong, it will?"

"Uh, uh," he whispered, moving his hands to frame her face. "Colin Murphy's law. The one that says, what I want, I take."

His mouth took hers as he fitted their bodies together in a close, erotic alignment that left no doubt about what Colin Murphy wanted.

2

A MONTAGE OF THE ACTIONS she ought to be taking flashed through Laine's head. She should tear her lips from Murphy's inflaming kiss, wrench her body away from the hands that stroked her back with languid familiarity. Maybe even accuse him of taking intolerable liberties. Instead she listened to a wanton little moan escape her parted lips, felt his sharp intake of breath and, an instant later, his tongue, as it slipped unchallenged into her mouth.

Murphy's lips were warm and soft, tempting her to respond rather than demanding it greedily. Laine welcomed the delicate invasion, unable—or unwilling—to resist such a gentle entreaty. But for a kiss that had happened so unexpectedly, it was packed with mind-numbing power and excitement. Far too much of both, Laine began to realize dimly, for a first kiss. Power and excitement like this could quickly get out of hand. She couldn't risk that, especially not with a man like Colin Murphy. Slowly, reluctantly, she drew back, resenting the separation even as she told herself she had no choice.

"Why did you do that?" Laine blurted out, belatedly aware of how inane the question sounded. But how could she think coherently when her brain cells had just been short-circuited? Seeing that Murphy seemed equally bemused made her feel a little better. If he had recovered quickly enough to come back with a glib retort, she'd have felt foolish, naive. As it was, he appeared to be carefully deliberating.

The kiss probably hadn't been all that great an idea, Murphy decided when he was finally able to think again. That, of course, was the problem. He had done it on impulse because he'd spent hours imagining what Laine would taste like, how she'd feel against him. And now he had the answer. She tasted and felt too damned good. A man could lose his head over temptation like that. Hadn't he just proven it?

Contrary to the reticent way he usually approached women, Murphy had come on to Laine like some macho clod. He might as well have gone the whole route, he thought disgustedly—beat his chest, yodeled like Tarzan and tossed her over his shoulder. He didn't delude himself that he fitted any of her requirements for a husband, wasn't all that sure he *wanted* to qualify. But he'd tipped his hand and gotten in line like all the other contenders. Why hadn't he waited, planned a less aggressive course? Now she had an excuse to write him off as one more reject.

Murphy's eyes narrowed as an idea came to him. Maybe it wasn't hopeless after all. He could use his impetuous behavior to recoup lost ground. There were always alternate ways to get what you wanted, if you were persistent enough.

Laine watched a lazy grin spread over Murphy's face. "Well, Sunshine, I figured I might as well make my pitch like everybody else and get it over with. Now that it's behind us, we can both relax and concentrate on being friends. I'll even volunteer my services in your man-hunt."

If she hadn't been able to read between the lines, Laine might have been hurt by his offhand dismissal of their stirring kiss. But she had felt the heavy thud of his heartbeat when their lips were joined, had heard his labored breathing in the aftermath. Regardless of what he might say now, Colin Murphy had been just as involved, just as affected by what they'd shared. She didn't understand why he'd offered such a lame excuse, or why he wanted to take part in her husband hunt. But she was going to find out. "What sort of help were you thinking of contributing to my project?"

"Oh, something along the lines of giving you tips from the male point of view. Men and women don't think alike. I can tell you how to avoid mistakes in handling the ones who look promising." He didn't mention that he'd also be playing devil's advocate, vetting the undesirables. There would be a lot of those. If Murphy had anything to say about it, something would be horribly wrong with every man except him.

It surprised him to discover how much he wanted Laine Randolph to give him all her time and attention. As a rule, he considered the machinations involved in courting a woman to be more effort than they were worth.

"I suppose I could use a second opinion," Laine ventured. "An objective evaluation of the competitors, so to speak."

"Exactly. And who better to aid the cause than a totally disinterested observer?" The little white lie slipped out so easily that Murphy found himself rationalizing that this one was for a good cause. Ordinarily, he detested lies and saw no reason for them. "The seminar doesn't begin until ten. Shall we meet for breakfast and map out a strategy?"

"Why not? Is seven too early?"

That time of morning was a crime against nature. It didn't exist as far as Murphy was concerned. "Seven is fine. I do some of my best work then." *If sleeping counted*, he amended silently. "See you in the dining room?"

She opened her mouth, reconsidered, nodded. Murmuring, "Until morning, then," she turned and drifted away, leaving him surrounded by the faint essence of her perfume.

Her voice had sounded husky, conjuring up images that magnified his already vivid fantasies. Tension banished Murphy's feigned composure as he watched Laine work her way across the room. Those fantasies were a long way from reality, he reminded himself, looking for the closest exit. He needed to escape.

Walking toward his room, Murphy absently unbuttoned his shirt. As he often did on the island, he thought of water as a way to relieve his body's tautness. His aches usually resulted from hours spent hunched over a drawing board, not from a sudden blazing hunger for one particular woman. At this time of year, the ocean in front of his house engulfed him like a warm, unresisting embrace. Bad analogy. Andy's sides would split if he could see Murphy now, consumed by lustful thoughts. Perfectly understandable, he supposed. Everyone knew that Murphy rarely got excited about anything.

He plunged his key into the lock. "God," he groaned. Why did every thought, every act, reinforce how much he wanted Laine Randolph? This morning he'd awakened in his own bed, reasonably content, unaware of her existence. Now here he stood, reeling from the tailspin Laine had thrown him into.

"Forget warm and embracing," Murphy grumbled, lobbing his hastily discarded clothes into a chair. He dug through a leather duffel for his swim trunks. An icy mountain lake was a better prescription for what ailed him tonight.

LAINE'S INTERNAL ALARM WOKE her at six, as it did every day. But rather than bounding out of bed, energized and eager to meet the day, she burrowed deeper beneath the covers. The warmth she sought eluded her until at last she sat up. A raucous serenade greeted her, courtesy of some early risers perched in the trees adjoining her deck. Laine smiled, remembering that she'd opted to leave the sliding door open last night because the mountain air had felt so crisply invigorating. This morning it was cold enough to make her shiver. Fully awake, thanks to the chorus and cool temperature, she rose and shrugged into her robe.

Laine had packed her car early yesterday morning looking forward to escaping Atlanta's unseasonable heat and humidity. What a difference a day and a few hundred miles made. She wasn't thinking of the weather now. She didn't understand why, or even how, Colin Murphy had diverted her from her purpose. Today she would pay closer attention to what Amanda Hunt said about pursuing goals.

After drifting along in an emotional limbo for a year, Laine had finally decided what she needed. Right away she began directing considerable energy toward attaining it. But last night's repeated reminders that she'd come here in search of a husband hadn't made any difference.

None of the men met her specifications, especially not Murphy. So why hadn't she sent him packing along with the rest? Why had she agreed to accept his help in her quest? She had suspected his motives as soon as he'd made the offer. It still didn't make sense that he'd wanted to help find her the perfect man. But curiosity overruled her suspicions. She looked forward to seeing him again.

Laine glanced at her small travel clock on the nightstand. She'd have to hurry her shower or be late for the breakfast meeting with Murphy. Thinking back to the tropical print shirt he'd worn yesterday, she selected a full skirt and matching camp shirt that sported bright turquoise and yellow flowers on a red background. It was a real eye-opener.

Murphy looked to be in desperate need of an eye-opener when she joined him at a few minutes past seven. He sat huddled over a cup of coffee, clutching it with both hands as if he hoped it might wake him up by osmosis.

"Did you know that a cup of tea has one-fifth the caffeine you'll get from that coffee?"

At the sound of her voice, he jumped. Some of the maligned brew sloshed out and scalded his fingers. "Ouch, dammit! You sneaked up on me."

"Murphy, walking straight toward you doesn't constitute *sneaking up.*" Laine plunked her tote into an empty chair and sat across from him. "You must have been asleep."

"Aaagh," he grunted, emptying the cup in several swallows.

"I don't think he's a morning person," she explained to their waitress in an exaggerated whisper. Laine gestured to the pot from which the fresh-faced young woman was about to refill Murphy's cup. "Better leave that. He's going to need a jump start."

"You early birds are a pain in the rear, you know that?" Murphy asked. "Always inflicting your obscene cheerfulness on the rest of us."

Laine smiled, finding his grumpiness oddly endearing. He looked miserable, and the little nick on his chin made her want to hug him for trying to shave when he was barely conscious. "I specifically remember asking if seven was too early for you."

Murphy kneaded his forehead. "And I specifically remember lying when I said no. I just don't remember why."

"We're supposed to plan a strategy for my manhunt, I believe is how you phrased it," she reminded him gently, sipping orange juice while she glanced at the menu. "You offered to help me."

"I can't imagine what possessed me to do that."

"Crawfishing already, Murphy?"

He took off his glasses and stared pensively at her for long moments. Laine was again struck by his extraordinarily beautiful eyes. An unusual, compelling blend of gold and green, they were the one remarkable feature in a face that could charitably be described as average. She carefully blocked out memories of how his lips had felt on hers, focusing instead on the thick medium brown hair that tended to curl, as it'd grown too long. His nose was also a shade too long, his jawline a little too square. No, she didn't see classic male beauty when she looked at Murphy. Laine appreciated a handsome masculine face as well as the next woman. It just didn't seem to matter much that Murphy didn't have one.

"No, Sunshine. I'm not crawfishing. It takes a lot to discourage me."

His morning-rough voice inspired a flood of inappropriate sensations. They were sitting in front of a sun-drenched window, but Laine felt a small chill slide down her spine. Yet inside she felt warm, fluid. Gazing into his enthralling eyes, she sensed that she had just acquired something more than a partner in her husband hunt.

Since Murphy seemed to be fully awake by the time they'd finished breakfast, Laine suggested a walk on one of the resort's many wooded trails. Not until they headed back to the meeting room did she realize that neither strategy nor eligible men had been among their conversational topics.

Laine was still reflecting on that when the seminar ended at noon. She had spent three hours with Murphy and their reason for getting together had rated only one brief mention. It was perplexing, but not entirely surprising. As he had from the first moment she met him, Colin Murphy was proving to be a major distraction.

Laine checked her watch. They had four hours before the next session. Subscribing to the theory that listeners' attention spans were finite, Amanda Hunt's seminars featured flexible schedules, each day's routine varying from the previous one. She had explained that people actually absorb more information if given time in between to reflect on it. Amanda's presentations were dynamic and full of group participation. Laine found them informative and helpful. Nevertheless, she was relieved to hear they didn't have to sit in a classroom all day. She much preferred being outdoors. Which was exactly where Amanda had held the second half of this morning's gathering.

Murphy sank down onto the low wooden bench Laine had claimed after Amanda dismissed them. "What do you want to do about lunch? We can either eat here at the lodge or find a restaurant somewhere close by." He evidently thought it was a foregone conclusion that they'd be sharing it. Laine didn't dispute his assumption.

She dug through the tote and extracted a newspaper she'd picked up while registering the previous afternoon. "I thought I might check out the Garbage Day celebration up in Beech Mountain. That's not far from here."

"What in God's name is Garbage Day? Or more to the point, why should anyone want to celebrate it?"

"Come on, Murphy, be a sport," Laine chided without looking up from an article she'd spotted in *The Mountain Times*. "Every year, the town has a parade in honor of the day they got their first garbage truck. It . . . sounds like fun."

"Sounds repulsive, if you ask me."

"No, listen. If we hurry we can make it up to Beech in time for the parade. After that we can collect a couple of bags of garbage so we can get into the festivities. It says here that the price of admission is a bag of trash. For that you get hot dogs, lemonade, music and games."

"I'm salivating already."

Laine ignored the sarcasm. She hopped up and pulled him to his feet. "Where's your spirit of adventure?"

"I lost it at an amusement park when I was twelve. On the *Drop of Doom*. Along with my lunch. A hot dog, I think. I haven't been very daring since."

"This won't hurt a bit," she promised, tugging him along in her path. "I'll drive. We'll get there faster that way."

Within minutes of darting into the lodge's kitchen to beg a pair of garbage bags, Laine sent her Wagoneer racing up Beech Mountain at a pace that would do a grand-prix driver proud.

Murphy tightened his seat belt for the third time. "Where did you learn to drive?"

"In Germany. Dawdle along on their autobahns and they'll run you right over. Relax. You're perfectly safe. I've never had a fender bender, much less a real accident." She patted his knee reassuringly.

"How about speeding tickets?" he asked, his voice sounding even tighter than before. "Had many of those?"

"I admit to a couple. But they weren't my fault."

"You were speeding, but it wasn't your fault?"

She lightened her touch on the accelerator a fraction. "What can I say? I'm a slave to horsepower. If it's there, I use it." Her partner had insisted she drive the company Jeep because she was going to scout a potential job on her way home. Privately Laine figured he didn't trust her driving her own car in the mountains.

Laine braked as they rounded a corner and came into the small town. "Oh, look. There's the fire engine all decorated with balloons. The parade must be getting started. See, I told you we'd make it in time." She wheeled the wagon onto the highway shoulder and parked. "Let's follow the action."

The parade didn't amount to much, she supposed. There were several amateurish floats, a few desultory marchers who were more concerned with having fun than keeping step and some children who'd trimmed their pets with colorful ribbons. But to Laine this was, in its own way, as delightful as her first visit to Disneyland. She had a natural curiosity, loved meeting people and finding out what interested them, what their lives were like.

During the short parade she'd spoken to a woman who, along with her husband, operated the local stables. Laine had tentatively accepted an invitation for herself and Murphy to go on a horse-drawn hayride one evening this week. And a wonderful old lady with gnarled, brown-spotted hands had urged them to stop by and see her quilt collection.

Technically she was on vacation, but even when Laine was working she frequently did this sort of thing. Soaking up local color helped her do business more efficiently. At least, that's what she'd told her partner when he'd speculated that she might have finished a day or two sooner. Laine never argued with him. Randy Williamson handled his responsibilities as skillfully as she did her own.

She took care of getting the jobs; Randy saw that they were carried out successfully. That was why Randolph and Randolph, R&R Inc., had gained the reputation of being one of the best demolition companies in the country. Both principals recognized their own, and the other's, strengths and capitalized on them.

"I think that's it for the parade," she said, taking Murphy's arm. Laine reached into the tote and retrieved two trash bags, passing one to Murphy. "It shouldn't take long to fill them." She pointed to the inevitable mess left behind by a crowd. "Then we can get our hot dogs and lemonade."

"This is like hunting for rotten Easter eggs," he complained, bending to snag a crumpled beer can.

"Maybe, but don't you remember Easter when you were little? All the time you were hunting the candy eggs, you really wanted to find the golden one. The one that could be exchanged for some fabulous treasure . . ."

Murphy straightened and smiled, a genuine smile with no trace of his usual derision. "Yeah. I do remember. I only found that golden egg once. I traded it for a top-notch mineral collection. In my seven-year-old eyes, it was the most beautiful, fascinating thing I'd ever seen."

The way that smile infused his harsh features with an expression of childlike wonder was a magical experience for Laine. It made her question what had turned him into a cynic. It also made her want to see that kind of smile again. Often.

Somehow that disturbed her more profoundly than anything else that had happened between them.

She quickly dismissed the image of herself as Colin Murphy's guide, teaching him to be more spontaneous and fun loving. If he wanted to be a grouch, it was his choice. And not her problem. Her determination renewed, Laine began cramming trash into her bag. Within minutes she and Murphy were able to pay their way into an area that was enclosed by a haphazardly built wooden fence. It needed the attention of some latter-day Tom Sawyer's paintbrush.

"You didn't tell me we could have paid our admission with money," Murphy grumbled after they claimed their hot dogs and lemonade. "I can't believe you had me scrounging around like a bag lady when it would have been simpler just to fork over two bucks. All this gourmet fare could have been ours without the sweat."

"Where's the fun in that? Food for garbage is a novel idea. It has real possibilities. Could even be a solution to the litter problem." Rearranging her full skirt, Laine stepped over the bench of a picnic table. She would have preferred sitting with some of the locals, but there hadn't been any empty spaces.

"Something tells me you never settle for the sublime when the ridiculous will serve better."

"What makes you say that?" she asked, nonplussed by the accuracy of his character analysis.

Murphy took his time chewing a bite of hot dog. "I guess because most people don't approach marriage from your angle."

"You don't believe most people see marriage as a goal to attain?"

"Maybe. But the majority just drift until the day when Prince Charming rides up on his white charger. Or in the case of men, muddle along until they find the lady whose dragons they want to slay. They sure as hell don't sign up for lessons on how to go about landing a mate."

Laine picked daintily at the excess bun, and tossed crumbs to a nearby bird. "Actually," she said, still looking at the bird, which had been joined by several others, "I didn't enroll to learn *how* to catch a man."

Murphy eyed her suspiciously. By now she could almost read the expression in his eyes, even though they were shielded by the dark glasses.

"Then why?"

She cleared her throat and told herself it didn't matter whether or not Murphy approved of her tactics.

"Several weeks ago my best friend's husband came here for a seminar. When Claire picked him up, she saw that a very high percentage of the participants were male. Knowing my search hadn't turned up anything interesting, she suggested that I enroll in a group. 'Prime pickings' is how Claire described what I would find at this place," Laine said, trying to imitate her friend's affected mountain accent.

"Ah, now I see. You came to actually catch a man, not to learn how." Laine was silent while he mulled over that revelation. "Tell me, how long have you been looking for Mr. Right?"

"For nearly a year." She flung her remaining hot dog to the birds. They attacked it avidly, as if they'd unearthed a giant worm.

"In all that time you haven't found ... there hasn't been anyone—"

"Oh, I've met lots of men. I already know lots of men. But it seems that if they meet some of the requirements, there's always one thing that makes them totally unacceptable." She'd bemoaned this complication often. Friends had begun accusing her of being naive, unrealistic. Laine had coolly informed them that she was cautious and thorough. Lately, some had hinted that she was only giving lip service to her goal of matrimony. But she did want to get married. It was only the selection process that was bothersome and unsatisfying.

"Sunshine, your paragon probably doesn't exist. You're doomed to failure. There are no perfect men. Or women."

His slightly amused tone almost veiled the scorn. But Laine heard it. Had a bad experience with a woman made him contemptuous of love and marriage? She remembered the recent television interview. Murphy had flatly, and not very tactfully, refused to divulge anything about his private life. He'd cut off the reporter's probe by insisting that his buildings said all anyone needed to know about him. Laine's interest had been piqued at the time. It was even more so now.

"Have you ever been married?" She was abruptly stricken by an even gloomier possibility. He could be married now.

"No. Never even came close." Murphy didn't react to her sigh of relief, and Laine was grateful for that. "It seems to bother my family and friends a lot more than it does me. You might say that's why I'm here."

"They sent you to find a wife?" Laine asked, not believing for a second that they shared a common goal. Murphy had to be in his mid to late thirties. He was fairly well-known and probably well-fixed. Despite his misanthropic tendencies, if he needed or wanted a wife, he'd have one by now.

"No, I'm not here to shop, but it's kind of a long story. You might appreciate the irony." He paused, as if deciding where to start. "Andy Keller and I have been best friends for as long as I can remember. We're as opposite as any two people you'll ever meet, but that's never mattered to us. Anyway, about ten years ago we started trading gag birthday gifts. Silly, useless things. Somewhere along the way it got out of hand. Now each of us tries to surpass the other with something as outlandish as it is unwelcome. The catch is that we have to use whatever we get."

That sounded like something she and Claire might dream up. She might even suggest it the next time they talked. "So Andy's gift to you was this goal-setting seminar?"

"Right. I got it last fall, but managed to put it off until finally he called Amanda and scheduled the week. Then he hit me with an accomplished fact."

"This doesn't seem like your typical sort of gag gift. I mean, anyone can benefit from learning how to set goals." Though she herself was guilty of distorting its intent, Laine felt the need to defend Amanda's program.

"The first thing this place had against it was that I don't like being anywhere but the beach. I think my body requires saltwater to function with any degree of efficiency. And I hate cozying up to people I don't know and have nothing in common with. Andy knows that as well as anyone. But lately he's developed some pretty asinine theories about the benefits of mountain air."

A quartet, amplified by the static-plagued sound system, began to sing a folk song. Laine raised her voice to be heard. "Why asinine? Why shouldn't mountain air be as beneficial as saltwater?"

Murphy shrugged. "Andy met his fiancée on a ski trip last year. The man's consumed with love, possessed by passion." He shook his head and chuckled, as if his friend were an object of pity. "I think he has some misbegotten notion that the same thing will happen to me. Pretty farfetched. But since he knows that, deal or not, I'd never go near snow, he sent me up here now."

"Well, it's only for five days," Laine said lightly. Suddenly she'd heard enough of Murphy's acerbic views on love and marriage. "Let's walk over to that shop across the street. I need to pick out a really tacky souvenir."

Like Murphy and his friend Andy, Laine and Claire had a long-established tradition. Neither of them ever visited the other without bringing a hostess gift. Both were relentless in their quest for state-of-the-art schlock.

Once they'd waded through the porch's clutter and were inside Fred's Mercantile, Purveyor of Fine Goods, Laine expressed her disappointment. "Oh, dear. All this stuff is *nice*. It will never do."

A black dog, part Labrador, almost opened one eye in silent condemnation. He clearly resented his nap being disturbed by customers.

Laine and Murphy inventoried a display of clever handcrafted birdhouses, then proceeded through the brooms and hardware. "There must be gourmets hiding out in these mountains," she speculated, pointing to shelves of champagne, wine, caviar, pâté and imported preserves.

Murphy read the sign, "If you can't find it here, you probably don't need it," and they both laughed.

They had reached a cooler containing bologna, cheese and canned pop. "Well, this is the sort of down-home flavor I'm looking for, but we never do food."

She snagged an employee and described something she'd seen recently, but hadn't taken time to buy. "It's a rest-room radio. A blue plastic, solid-state, full-circuit, tissue-dispensing radio that plays the Georgia Tech fight song. For complete private enjoyment. With little black-and-gold helmets on the tissue."

The clerk and Murphy looked equally appalled.

"We might be able to find something that's semi-tacky," the clerk said.

"I thought you were only joking," Murphy chimed in. "You wouldn't seriously consider giving away anything that rude, would you?"

"In a flash. It's what we live for."

"Maybe you should check some of the places farther down the mountain," the clerk suggested hopefully.

"Good idea," Laine agreed, grabbing Murphy. "We'd better hurry if we don't want to be late for this afternoon's session."

"I hope my heart can stand the excitement," he said, straightening his shoulders in a show of bravery.

Laine didn't comment on his allusion to her driving skills. She'd make her point in a more active way. Everyone knew you could get down a mountain faster than you could go up.

LAINE LISTENED INTENTLY when Amanda Hunt talked to them about working toward the goal that was currently most important in your life plan. If attaining it was crucial, you had to concentrate all your drive, every ounce of energy toward the pursuit of that one objective. You had to be single-minded. And you had to persevere.

She explained the technique of imaging, picturing yourself getting exactly what you want, when you want it.

Laine tried to image herself in a gorgeous satin-and-lace wedding gown, floating down the aisle to join futures with her perfect match. The image refused to stay in focus.

What kept recurring was a picture of Murphy and her sharing a cozy, candlelight dinner at a remote mountain inn. They lingered over dessert, talking softly, laughing easily. Murphy's dark glasses had disappeared. He caressed her, tenderly and often, but only with his eyes. Laine was relieved. She already felt so warm, so restless that she might dissolve at the touch of his hands. Later, when they were alone, she would show Colin Murphy that he wasn't the only one who could work magic.

Laine's renegade image proved to be remarkably accurate—until the evening's conclusion. Murphy left her with only a gossamer trailing of his fingers down her cheek and over her lips.

She told herself it was more than enough.

Caressing her cheek wasn't enough for Murphy. All day he had reminded himself that he had to proceed cautiously with Laine. Amanda Hunt's instructions on imaging had wreaked havoc with his good intentions. His fantasies had run wild and driven him crazy. Something told him that tonight even swimming in a frigid lake wouldn't take his mind off where he wanted to be.

He wasn't certain where he and Laine were headed, or even where he wanted them to go. His body didn't seem at all uncertain, he thought, reacting to its insistent message with wry humor. But Murphy knew himself well enough to recognize there was more going on here than sexual attraction.

If that was the case, he wouldn't want to spend every minute with Laine, to find out everything he could about her. He wouldn't be plotting ways to divert her from her goal of finding a husband. Or trying to involve himself in whatever occupied her at the moment, even a scatterbrained garbage hunt. No, a man interested only in quick physical satisfaction would push his advantage and not worry about tomorrow.

He did have an advantage. Laine obviously found something that she liked about him. She had spent far more time with him than with any of the other men present. Though he couldn't imagine why, Murphy wasn't about to question his good fortune.

He crawled into bed, staring thoughtfully at the shadows on the ceiling. He might not know where all this was heading, but he sure as hell was thinking about tomorrow. And the next day. After that, there was next week to worry about. Laine Randolph didn't know it yet, but when she left North Carolina, Colin Murphy was going to be hot on her trail.

3

"WHAT'S ON THE AGENDA for this afternoon?" Murphy inquired of Laine when he'd caught up with her on their way out of the conference room. "After lunch, that is. I'm starved."

She avoided mentioning that he had not only missed his morning meal, but had staggered bleary-eyed into the eight o'clock meeting twenty minutes late. Early was not his best time of day. "A few of us were talking at breakfast. And since all afternoon is free, we decided to play a round of golf."

The grimace conveyed his feelings without words. "That's better than scavenging garbage, I guess, but just barely."

Laine laughed at his expression, promptly forgetting her early-morning resolution. During a restless night, she'd made up her mind to give the eligible men a second chance. She needed to remember that she was here for a reason—the most crucial current goal in her life plan, to quote Amanda's words. Unless she stopped spending time with Murphy exclusively, she wouldn't make any progress toward finding a suitable husband.

"Does that look of boredom and disgust mean you won't be joining in the fun?"

"Put it this way. I don't agree with the saying that golf is the most fun you can have with your clothes on."

If anyone else had said it, she would have found the adage amusing. Coming from Murphy, and accompanied by a sizzling look, it made Laine glance down to be sure she was still wearing the modest white cotton shirtwaist. "There are plenty of people who don't share your opinion." It was a good thing she didn't sound as excited as she felt.

"Fun is not whacking away at a little white ball so you can chase it all over the landscape," he asserted vehemently. "Golf's a stupid game."

Laine shrugged. As a rule she figured everyone was entitled to his own opinion, even a negative one. She just didn't waste much time with people like that. But Murphy's cranky pessimism was a challenge to her, especially since she suspected much of it was contrived. She couldn't resist needling him about it. "What's your idea of fun?"

"Stick around and you'll find out."

She did a double take. He wasn't even looking at her. Maybe he hadn't meant it to sound like an erotic suggestion. But to Laine it sounded like a promise so sensual that little tremors raced through her like wildfire, coming to rest deep and low inside her. These flashes of awareness struck suddenly and at the oddest moments. As an engineer, she tended to think in precise terms. Yet every time Laine tried to analyze Murphy's mystifying allure, she drew a blank. It simply *was*, contrary to all logic and reason.

But just because their affinity was undeniable didn't mean she had to act on it. Murphy hadn't made any overt moves since his audacious kiss that first night. His explanation for kissing her was logical, even though she had a problem accepting the fact he'd wanted to "get it over with." It was probably all in her head anyway. Maybe approaching thirty made a woman's hormones turn traitorous.

All at once, Laine needed to put some distance between her and Murphy. If that meant skipping lunch, so be it. She veered away from the dining room and started up the stairs, tossing a casual invitation over her shoulder. "Well, if you change your mind about the golf game, we're teeing off at two." Half of her hoped he'd be there while the other part mentally crossed her fingers that he would be a no-show. Muttering to herself that she shouldn't care one way or the other, Laine raided the tote for a granola bar.

When she reached her room she went straight to the small refrigerated bar for a soft drink to wash the snack down. They were poor substitutes for the chef's salad she'd been anticipating, but sometimes sacrifices had to be made in the name of self-preservation. Laine paused in midbite, exasperated that Murphy had her thinking in those terms. Forcefully crunching down on the bar, she ignored that thought. So she felt twinges of attraction to the man. That didn't mean she couldn't overcome them.

Twinges, she repeated in silent accusation. If these were twinges, she'd hate to get hit by a full-fledged attack.

Shortly before two, Laine wrestled to extract her clubs from the Jeep. Its cargo section was overflowing with tools of the trade so that all her personal gear had to be crammed into the backseat.

"Need any help?"

His drawled question accompanied by cleated footsteps on the paved parking lot put an end to Laine's vacillation about Murphy's presence or lack of it. Whether it was wise or not, she was glad to see him here. In her opinion, he needed to play more. If he could put aside his dislike of golf for the afternoon, she'd see that he had a good time.

A second inspection of the available men had proved no more encouraging than the first. There was no reason for her to feel guilty about having fun with Murphy.

Without waiting for a response to the offer of help, he tucked his glasses in his hip pocket and shouldered her golf bag. For someone who supposedly detested the game, he seemed anxious to get started. "Couldn't resist the lure of the links, I see."

"Couldn't resist."

Laine's footsteps almost faltered when he sent her that hot look again, along with a smile that would make a prudent woman run for cover. Impetuously, she decided that prudence was overrated. Fueled with reckless confidence, she returned his smile and led him toward the clubhouse.

Murphy watched, charmed, as Laine sailed into the midst of the waiting group and proposed that they lay a small wager. Since there were eight of them, she suggested a competition among four teams, with the highest scoring pair buying drinks at happy hour that night. Someone else came up with an idea for pairing that would make the contest as equal as possible. He almost laughed aloud after a comparison revealed Laine to have the lowest average. He couldn't have planned it better.

"I don't play golf," Murphy said, trying to sound properly apologetic for his shortcomings. "I have no idea how high I might shoot." His claim was only a slight distortion of the facts. He didn't like to play and did so rarely. But if motivated he could turn in a fairly respectable score. He was rarely motivated. Murphy hadn't been joking about his assessment of the game as stupid. But as his behavior the past several days indicated, he'd go to extreme lengths to be with Laine Randolph.

With a bit of maneuvering, he ensured that he and Laine would be last. He didn't want anyone behind them, and it was easy enough to convince the others that he didn't want to hold them up with his amateurish play.

As Laine shaded her eyes with one hand and watched the other pairs tee off, Murphy watched her. She was wearing a bright yellow split skirt, matching yellow-and-white-striped shirt and white golf shoes. It was a demure outfit that, incongruously, spawned vivid erotic fantasies. It was going to be a long afternoon.

When it was their turn, Laine watched Murphy tee up the ball. His jeans had been worn until they were soft and nearly colorless. They defined several wholly masculine attributes that nice girls would pretend not to notice. Laine stared anyway. *Women* were allowed an occasional guilty pleasure. A wide, scuffed leather belt anchored the jeans below his lean waist. A snug white polo shirt clung to surprisingly broad shoulders and outlined the swell of his biceps. There had been no clue that the slouchy clothes he'd worn up to this point concealed such a sleek, disturbingly potent package.

She'd admired his intelligence and wit before they'd even met. And after knowing him a few days, she found that his quirky personality made the more agreeable, socially adept men seem bland and inconsequential. Now she also had to contend with this incipient physical attraction. It simply wasn't fair.

Yanked out of her reverie by his wild swing, Laine frowned when Murphy topped his first shot and it dribbled to the side after traveling about twenty yards. "Watch the ball until you hit it," she instructed, resorting to bossy benevolence to regain her equilibrium. "I'll keep track of where it goes."

"Then we're both in for a long afternoon, Sunshine."

A wry chuckle followed his prediction, and Laine felt as if she'd missed a joke. Undaunted she pulled out a driver and took up her coaching duties. "Now pay attention to my stance." She squared up to the tee. "Be sure your feet and shoulders are in line. Relax, make your grip firm, but remember you're not out to choke the club. Most importantly, don't take your eyes off the ball." She connected with a solid shot, satisfied when the ball landed about a hundred and thirty yards down the fairway. "And did you notice my follow-through?"

"Oh, yeah. I noticed."

All of Laine's feminine instincts went on full alert. Golf swing forgotten, she turned, struck by the edge she heard in his voice. He'd put on his glasses; brilliant sun had darkened the lenses to near black. But she didn't have to see his eyes. She could feel the impact of their intensity all the way to her toes. Laine shivered in spite of the fine layer of moisture that glazed her body.

After a long, nerve-stretching silence, she said huskily, "Your shot, Murphy."

He studied her for another moment, then let out an audible breath and ambled off toward his ball. Her eyes followed his progress down the fairway, noted the lazy play of hip and leg as they moved in fluid harmony. She imagined muscles flexing, extending, and her fingers tingled with heat that spread quickly to other, more intimate places. What was wrong with her? Indulging in sexual fantasies while standing on a golf course was not normal behavior for Laine. Maybe the rush of heat was caused by sunstroke.

Shaking herself from the trance, she made it to the cart. Her legs had turned weak and boneless, her hands damp and tremulous. It was only the first hole. Could she survive this refined torture for eight more? No way. She ought to whip the ridiculous-looking vehicle around and speed away as fast as its anemic battery would carry her. Instead she steered it down the path with painstaking slowness, as if guiding it required all her skill and concentration.

Just as she coasted to a stop, Murphy was preparing to drive. He shifted back and forth several times, alternating feet, seeking the proper balance. From her storehouse of trivia she recalled a survey about what women first noticed about a man. Buns. Here, now, she understood why. Laine swallowed a helpless moan.

Turning, he asked, "You okay, Sunshine? You look flushed."

"Sunstroke," she murmured distractedly. "Nothing serious." *Murphy is a sexless android*, she tried repeating silently while she stared at the horizon. She'd read that was a way to orient yourself when you felt unsteady. Trying to sound brisk and controlled, she apologized. "Sorry if I interrupted you."

He lifted one shoulder in dismissal. With a knowing grin, he swiveled back around and sent the ball sailing. While he was a long way from tournament competition, it was a much better shot than the first. Seeming neither surprised nor pleased, he folded himself into the seat beside Laine. "Can you drive with, um, sunstroke, or do you want me to take over?"

He was close—arm, hip, leg brushing against hers. She felt warmth and rough textures, smelled a spicy scent that was so faint she had to lean closer and inhale deeply to make sure.

"Laine?"

"What? Oh, uh, no. I mean, yes. I can drive." To prove her point, she stomped on the pedal and they shot forward, lurching and weaving like a sailor coming off a three-day shore pass. After they'd swerved onto the fairway, Murphy nudged her foot aside and steadied their erratic course.

"It's not that I have any great reverence for the real estate, you understand. But I do value my neck."

Enough is enough! Giving herself a lecture on self-discipline, Laine struggled to regain command of herself and the cart. For the next seven holes she suppressed her attraction to Murphy as successfully as she avoided sand traps and water hazards. She gave incessant instructions, praising him as she would an obedient puppy if he followed them, scolding if he didn't. He was showing consistent improvement until one of his tee shots took a high, arcing flight and after a single bounce, ricocheted into the rough.

Since the resort had literally been carved out of the woods, its golf course was bounded on both sides by a dense stand of trees. On the side where Murphy's ball had disappeared, pink-and-white rhododendrons sculpted the fairway's contour.

Laine had expected one of his typically acerbic comments, but he looked almost smug. Before she could suggest that he take a one-shot penalty and forget searching for it, Murphy had slipped behind a bank of flowering shrubs. Gamely she followed.

After about five fruitless minutes of scouring the undergrowth, she was ready to give up and go back. She should have done it sooner.

Murphy stood directly in front of her, pinning her with that look of his. She told herself he wasn't really large and imposing. He was just close. He was also devastating, dangerous and ... Laine broke off all the alliteration. But it was too late. The next word reverberated inside her head. "Oh, Lord," she sighed. This was no affinity, no slight attraction she felt for him. It was desire, burning pure and hot.

This couldn't be happening to her. She, who during the past two years had preferred the art of keeping men at a safe distance, was melting because a pair of tawny eyes was moving over her like a slow, arousing caress. Laine started a backward retreat, but after only one step the boughs of a white pine tree brushed her shoulder. She was trapped. "I wish you wouldn't do this, Murphy."

His gaze lifted, met hers. "This?" he asked, spanning the short distance to lay his fingertips against the pulse that hammered wildly in the side of her neck.

Laine's tongue froze; she couldn't force out the protest she wanted to make.

"This?" His thumb rubbed lightly over her parted lips.

She shook her head, but that only increased the friction, deepened the contact. Blood coursed through her veins in a heated rush, making her feel light-headed.

"Or this?" He nuzzled aside her collar so his tongue could trace her collarbone.

When his index finger trailed down the front opening of her shirt, Laine whispered, "No," and grasped his wrist. Her thumb measured the heavy pulse-beat there.

"No?" His hand rotated, breaking her hold, closing on hers, guiding it to his chest. "What do you wish I'd do, Sunshine?"

WHAT DID SHE WISH Murphy would do? Laine asked herself as she set out on a solitary walk in the woods at twilight. She'd been able to avoid answering his question that afternoon. A noisy foursome had rescued her, shouting and laughing until she and Murphy had had no choice but to come out and finish playing the hole. Mercifully only the ninth remained and they had hurried through that one. Their conversation was limited and strained.

She'd wanted to forego the happy hour that followed, but since it was her idea to begin with, skipping out would have seemed like sour grapes. Murphy had accepted their losing score with a surprisingly gallant display of goodwill. "My fault," he informed everyone, then insisted on footing the bill for several rounds of drinks. Served him right, she thought churlishly. It was his fault that their combined scores were so high. Laine liked to win.

She bent to pick up one of the huge pinecones scattered about the trail. It was larger than her hand and the faintly resinous aroma pleased her. To Laine, the smell of pine meant Georgia. Home. She'd been eighteen, and without roots, when she and her sister had started college in Atlanta. It had quickly become the home they'd always wanted. Neither had ever intended to leave.

Maureen had enrolled at Emory for undergraduate, then medical school, while Laine attended Georgia Tech. They'd both built successful careers and the future looked promising. They had thought the world was theirs until Maureen...

As if prodded by an unseen force Laine took off down the path at a furious pace. She absolutely refused to

dwell on the past any longer. She had to go forward.
That was why she was here.

Just over a year ago, a vague but expanding discontent had begun plaguing Laine, a void that ached to be
filled. She had finally decided it must be a husband, and
eventually children, that were missing. Thus her
search.

That brought her back to Murphy, or more pointedly, what she was going to do about him. With the genius of hindsight she supposed she ought to have
recognized him as trouble and steered clear of him from
day one. Perhaps even before that. She recalled how
he'd gotten inside her head just from watching him on
that television interview. Since then, at odd moments
Laine had inexplicably found herself thinking about
both the man and what he'd said.

Preoccupied, she clenched her hand and one of the
needlelike tips of a scale punctured her palm. "Ouch,"
she yelped, tossing down the pinecone. Illogically, she
damned Murphy for the mishap. But that didn't solve
the problem of how to handle him and the aberrant
craving he inspired.

The solution was no clearer two nights later when
Laine was getting ready for a farewell pool-and-patio
party. In the intervening time she'd gnawed on the issue like a dog with a bone. Her only action had been
the cowardly one of avoiding Murphy entirely. She had
even sneaked off last night and gone on the hayride
alone. It hadn't been much fun.

Laine took out an electric-blue swimsuit and complementing cover-up. Maybe she was worrying needlessly. Tomorrow morning was the last session and everyone would be leaving right after lunch. There would be no reason to ever see Colin Murphy again. Here in the insular vacationlike setting, they had refrained from sharing any meaningful details of their day-to-day life. That hadn't stopped her from wondering about how Murphy lived, and where, but finding out wouldn't have been wise. The less she knew, the quicker she could forget him.

Hands on hips, Laine frowned at her mirrored reflection. Had this bikini always been cut so daringly high on the legs and so low over her stomach? Had she really bought something that exposed so much of her breasts? Or was she just more conscious now of her own body—as conscious as she was of Murphy's? Her last thought before slipping on the rose-colored gauze cover-up and picking up her tote was to wonder how much Murphy's swim trunks would reveal.

MURPHY WAS IN A SURLY MOOD. He sprawled indolently in one of the webbed poolside chairs, legs stretched out in front of him, ankles crossed. Fidgety feet, clad in battered yellow running shoes, were his only exterior sign of life. He hoped his pose would discourage any unwanted socializers. All this rah-rah togetherness could be toxic. Unless he was with Laine. But she had spent the past two days dodging his every attempt to come near her. Just when they were beginning to get close. "Damn!" he swore softly. Trying to understand women was a pain. Which was why he didn't usually bother. The change in his life-style after his thirtieth birthday had effectively relieved him of that burden.

As soon as he'd graduated from Princeton and begun making money, Murphy had started socking away every spare dollar. He had always known what he wanted. In order to get it, he'd had to go with one of the big architectural firms and live in Chicago. But as soon as his work achieved a measure of recognition, he left to establish his own firm in Atlanta, closer to where he wanted to be. For the next few years he concentrated on becoming successful enough to leave it all behind.

Several years ago his dream had become reality. Murphy had bought a tiny speck of an island off the Georgia coast and retired. Oh, it wasn't really retirement. He kept the firm, taking on a managing junior partner. And he kept on designing—his first love. But now he only chose the most interesting projects and left the nuts-and-bolts execution to employees. He handled the initial client meetings, preliminary scouting of building sites and occasional visits during construction.

Early in his career he'd learned that in order to create, to consistently produce worthwhile and satisfying designs, he had to remove himself from the fast-paced, upwardly mobile urban competitiveness that characterized his profession. For an emotionally self-sufficient person like Murphy, the beauty of living on an island was that it insisted on his separateness, held the world at bay. It didn't, however, offer much in the way of feminine companionship. After so long, he had convinced himself he preferred it that way.

He liked his life the way it was. After all, if a female were around, she'd turn up her nose when the urge struck him to eat sardines straight from the can...in bed...naked. Or she would get in a dither when he just moved to a different room rather than change the sheets. And he could imagine the womanly outrage that would erupt on nights when he decided to draw or play the piano until dawn, then sleep past noon.

But from the moment he'd nicknamed her Sunshine, Murphy had been able to envision Laine Randolph in his bright, airy island home. He'd designed the unique house to suit his tastes and needs, but its spaciousness and light could easily accommodate her brilliant smile and spirited outlook on life. The house would welcome her. And so would he.

The sudden quieting of his feet was the only indication that Murphy had seen Laine step onto the patio and flash her trademark smile at one of the men. *Enjoy yourself, Sunshine. Later tonight, it's my turn.* He got up and sauntered toward the buffet.

It was almost a relief when one of the women in their group started a conversation as they helped themselves to smoked salmon. He could stand a diversion from Laine and that filmy pink thing that didn't quite hide what it was supposed to. Within minutes he was almost relaxed. Talking to the friendly, no-nonsense lady whose Seattle marketing firm occupied three floors of a building he had designed didn't turn him into a bundle of nerves or make him hot in all the wrong places.

Murphy hadn't worn a swimsuit at all, Laine mused, absently running her fingers up and down a glass of iced tea. Maybe he viewed swimming with the same disdain he showed for other outdoor activities. He was dressed in the familiar uniform of jeans, but this evening he'd tucked in a red-and-green-plaid shirt, its sleeves rolled up midway on his tanned forearms. He looked even better than he had on the golf course.

She glanced away, then relented, watching from the corner of her eye as he listened interestedly to what Joy, the woman from Seattle, was saying to him. It must be fascinating. They had been talking for ages. Ridiculous, irrational and petty as it was, Laine felt a tiny niggle of resentment.

"What's the verdict after you've gotten to know him?"

Grateful for the interruption, Laine turned to Amanda. There wasn't any doubt that she was asking about Murphy. "Crabby, cynical, perverse."

Amanda laughed. "And?"

"Bright, funny, challenging," she admitted grudgingly, wishing she hadn't discovered the latter.

Amanda bent to scoop up a Siamese cat that twined itself around her legs. "Is it those character traits you're trying so hard not to look at tonight?"

Laine's head jerked up and her startled gaze collided with Amanda's. "Is it that obvious?"

"Only to someone who recognizes the symptoms. Take it from one who's been there."

Because Laine had felt a compatibility with Amanda from the beginning, she didn't hesitate to confide. "You know about that embryonic stirring when you first meet? A visceral reaction you can't quite describe, but, boy, do you feel it!"

She barely paused for Amanda's soft murmur of agreement. "You start paying attention to things that you've never noticed about other men. His body, how it's put together, the way he moves."

"Yes," she heard Amanda whisper, "I know all about that."

"His voice," Laine went on tightly, "though it's kind of rough and raspy, gets under your skin. You hear it, feel it, in your sleep." She heard Murphy laugh, the sound distinctive because of its infrequence. She forced herself not to look toward the other end of the pool, unable to face confirmation that he'd defected. It was what she had encouraged him to do, but confronting the evidence of it was unexpectedly depressing. "And those *looks*. Good heavens," she said, laughing a bit nervously. "You must think I've made one-too-many trips to the bar." Laine drank deeply from the tall tea glass. "I don't know why I'm raving on and on about this, as though it were some earth-shattering event. It's just chemistry. It'll go away."

"I said that, too."

"And did it? Go away, I mean?"

"Afraid not."

"So what did you do about it?"

"Well," Amanda said cheerfully, "I told myself I was a big girl and that I could take the edge off my sexual attraction by going to bed with him."

"I can see how that might be a solution," Laine allowed, certain it wasn't the answer for her. She was attracted to Murphy on too many levels beyond the physical. But maybe . . . "How long did it take?"

Amanda shook her head. "Three years, a wedding and one baby later, I still think he's the sexiest thing that ever put on a pair of jeans." Smiling at Laine's muffled whimper, she added, "I don't anticipate changing my mind anytime soon."

"Damn!" Laine whispered. "I think it would be more reassuring if you had just lied."

"Sorry I couldn't tell you what you wanted to hear," Amanda said, standing. "But I'm sure you'll find a way to work it out." She gave Laine an encouraging pat on the arm. "Guess I'd better play hostess and mingle."

Laine foraged through the tote for her oversize sunglasses. Hiding behind them, she could observe the action without anyone knowing that her target was Murphy. It was only fair. She suspected he used dark lenses more to mask his feelings and reactions than because he needed them for correction.

A small group had joined her at the glass-topped table. She listened to them with one ear in order to make appropriate comments. But like her eyes, her thoughts were focused on Murphy.

He was still at the buffet, and so was Joy, but they had been joined by a crowd of hungry guests. The party was open not only to Amanda's seminar participants, but also to those attending other meetings and people who were vacationing at the resort.

If she hadn't heard Murphy's repeated avowals that he detested this sort of gathering, she'd have guessed he was enjoying himself. How strongly had she wished he'd relent and be more receptive to experiences and people? Now that he appeared to be doing precisely that, she felt neglected.

At that moment he looked up and reality struck like a bolt of lightning. He hadn't defected at all. He'd just fallen back temporarily. Tonight the wait was over. Laine told herself there was no logical basis for that conclusion. But the atavistic female core of her knew, and it shrieked for her to raise some defenses. She stirred restlessly in her chair, but couldn't look away.

Murphy snagged a bottle of beer from one of the circulating waiters' trays. His thumb and index finger wrapped around the neck and carried it to his mouth. Laine watched the shift of throat muscles as he swallowed, swallowing herself when his tongue flicked over his lips. She had never realized that the simple act of a man drinking could be so sensual it made her mouth dry. But then, Colin Murphy had reeducated her about several things.

Laine's gaze followed as he lowered the bottle. His hands had fascinated her when she first noticed them. Tanned, lean, long-fingered, they would move with skill and sensitivity over a drawing board, piano keys or her.... She drained the tea and wished it were something stronger.

A clamorous game of water volleyball churned up the pool, splashing anyone who ventured close. Laine was only marginally aware of the noise and cutthroat style of play. Her attention was riveted on Murphy's mouth. He bit into some kind of oozy hors d'oeuvre, chewed, then licked his fingertips.

She couldn't take any more. She had to either cool off or melt the plastic on her chair. Forgetting the skimpy suit, she stripped off her cover-up and strode purposefully to the pool's edge. Poised to dive, she stole one last look at the man who was doing such crazy things to her libido.

Murphy stood apart from the crowd now, his beer in one hand, a chicken drumette in the other. When he noticed her, both hands dropped to his side; she could see the rise and fall of his chest.

"God!" That one word was all Murphy could say, and it was whispered. He'd seen beautiful women in skimpy bathing suits before. Seeing Laine was like being struck by lightning. Their eyes locked. Neither moved.

They were separated by the length of the pool, but powerful nonverbal messages crackled across the distance as if it didn't exist. Laine's lips parted. He saw her wet them, welcoming, beckoning. He couldn't wait another heartbeat. She was his and he was going after her.

Eyes unwavering, Murphy took one step toward her, a second, then another.

He kept advancing until he walked straight into the shallow end of the pool.

4

"MURPHY, SLOW DOWN," Laine protested, trying without success to pry his fingers from their lock on her wrist. Still dripping from his ignominious dunking, he hauled her up the stairs in furious silence. At least she presumed he was furious. He hadn't said a word yet. Just discarded his chicken and beer on the pool apron, then propelled himself out of the water with a single lithe motion and came stalking after her. Oblivious to the shocked stares and teasing catcalls, he had dragged her off the patio so fast she only had time to grab her cover-up on the run.

"Where are we going?" She knew the question was superfluous and his quick over-the-shoulder glare confirmed it. His room would be the only logical destination for an infuriated, soaked man whose shoes squished with every step. "Why are you towing me along?" This time he rolled his eyes, as if pleading for a higher authority to spare him another imbecilic question.

Laine conceded the point in silence. She knew what was on his mind. The same thing was on hers. Her sensory receptors had come alive the moment he looked at her from across the pool. They were still vibrating because Murphy intended to do more than just send signals. That much had been evident from the moment his usual lethargy erupted into swift, decisive action.

He unlocked the door and thrust her in ahead of him. From behind, his hands landed on her shoulders and squeezed once. "Stay put while I change clothes."

Laine whirled around to object to the quietly imperious command. "Look, Murphy, you've no—" She halted in midsentence because she'd lost her train of thought. He was unbuttoning his shirt, each move of his hands widening the wedge of exposed flesh. His upper chest was a tantalizing combination of tanned skin and fine, gold-tipped brown hair that tapered into a smooth, lean midriff. Lower, beneath his navel, the pattern narrowed before disappearing into wet denim.

"I've no what, Sunshine?" he asked, tugging the shirt out of his jeans.

With a guilty start, Laine forced herself to look up. His voice sounded more composed than she'd expected, and considerably calmer than her churning insides felt. She looked around the room, searching out a neutral, nonstimulating view because now he was peeling off the shirt. It made little sucking noises as it separated from his skin. Unnerved, Laine shook out the frothy bit of rose-colored gauze she clutched in her fist and hastily tugged it over her head.

"No? . . ." he prompted again, tossing the shirt through the bathroom doorway. It landed in the tub with a splat, and he yanked down a towel, using it on his hair.

"Uh, no right to drag me up here like an unruly child. No right to act as if your plunge was my fault."

"Do you think I'm in the habit of walking fully clothed into swimming pools? That I'd get my favorite shoes wet on purpose?" He kicked out of the soggy Nikes and gave them a mournful look. "Of course it's your fault."

Laine bristled at the accusation. "I realize that you don't like to swim, but—"

"Where did you get that idea?"

"I assumed when you weren't dressed for swimming that you didn't like it any better than you do other physical activities." Her lips tightened when she saw his crafty grin.

"I like to swim. Do it almost every day for at least an hour. But I prefer it in the ocean." With languid rotations, he rubbed the terry cloth over his chest and arms, then looped it around his neck. "Without clothes."

Laine felt the prickle of gooseflesh, at odds with a rising inner heat. She gave up trying not to look at his bare torso. It was right at eye level, she rationalized, so making a production of looking elsewhere would only draw attention to her growing uneasiness.

Daily swimming explained the shoulders, the well-defined pecs, the sinewy arms. She couldn't picture Murphy working out, so she credited his board-flat midsection, streamlined hips and tight backside to good genes.

"You like to swim in the ocean at midnight, Sunshine? Naked and uninhibited?"

The timbre of his voice flowed over Laine, flooding her with images of them together, caressed by warm seawater. "I—" She cleared her throat. "I've never—"

She was almost thirty years old and Murphy could make her stammer like a teenage virgin. She resented it. And she wanted him. Desire grew like an unbearable thirst, magnified because she didn't dare quench it.

Laine told herself she could avoid temptation if she got away from him, got back to the security of a crowd. Fortified by that conviction, she took several brisk steps toward the door. "Why don't I leave you to finish changing and see you back at the party?"

"Maybe later," he said, closing the small distance she'd managed to put between them. "Not right now." With almost no effort Murphy pulled her against him. "Now, I'm going to kiss you."

As she had been the first time, Laine was awed by the inherent magic she felt at the merest touch of Colin Murphy's mouth. It captured her, drew her in, and she wanted to revel in it forever. But he wasn't satisfied with a few whisper-light brushes. Deepening the kiss, he coaxed her lips to part by opening his own.

Her fluttery gasps mingled with Murphy's heavier, deeper breathing. He rested his hips against the dressing-room vanity and fitted Laine into the V formed by his legs. His hands shaped her waist, then relaxed to ride low on her hips. Reality again receded and Laine clung to his shoulders, her anchor in a storm-driven swell of emotion.

His tongue gently grazed the corners of her mouth and painted the outline of her upper lip before sliding inside with a bold stroke. Nimble, skillful, it sought, flirted, seduced. Laine weakened, turning into his willing victim. But she wasn't passive. She met the daring invasion, and gratified by his responsive groan, made her own passionate demands.

A rough sound of satisfaction rumbled deep in his chest when her tongue swirled around his; unintelligible words poured into her mouth. Murphy closed the angle of his outstretched legs, urging her into a more evocative embrace. Only seconds after he arched her against his arousal, Laine became abruptly, chillingly aware that she was rubbing against soaked jeans.

"Oh, Murphy," she whispered plaintively, breaking the intimate bond. Her hands trailed down his arms. "There are at least a dozen reasons why we shouldn't do this."

He leaned his forehead against hers. "And twice that many why we should. If I could talk, I'd list them." He kissed her temple, her eyelid, her ear. "But I can't even think." Shrugging the towel away, he took both her hands in his and transferred them to his shoulders again. "Come here, Laine. Stop thinking. And for God's sake, stop talking."

Their kiss began where the last one had left off. And this time, Laine abandoned herself to the hot, sweet wonder of it. Her hands sinuously charted the breadth of his shoulders, the back of his neck, then wandered lower. Murphy's back was such a delicious study in masculine contrasts. Soft skin, cool from the water, stretched sleekly over ridges of hard muscle. With the pads of her fingers, she stroked the shallow groove that followed his spine from neck to base. He sucked in a ragged breath when Laine combed her fingers through a small patch of silky hair in the hollow there.

While she luxuriated in her exploratory journey, Murphy was busy with his own discoveries. The thigh-length cover-up was no obstacle to his questing hands. Laine felt the play of his fingers on the bare skin of her hip, just above the bikini bottom. After his thumbs had drawn teasing circles inside the rings that joined the front and back of her suit, they smoothed up past her waist and toyed with the clip that fastened the top.

Before she could stop him, the clip separated and her breasts molded to his chest. Murphy released his hands and bowed his back away from her. The strapless bikini top landed on the floor with barely a sound and his foot nudged it away.

"Soft," he murmured, as his hands glided over her with agonizing slowness. "Ah, Sunshine." His teeth closed on her earlobe with a gentleness that hinted at an almost savage restraint.

Laine's nails sank into his back when his hands framed her sides, thumbs delicately sweeping the undercurves of her breasts. His implicit promise tightened her nipples against the airy fabric. She yearned to arch into his palm, plead with him to move his hand higher, touch her harder. The plea was unnecessary. His thumb and forefinger joined to skillfully ply her nipple to an almost painful tautness.

"I want to kiss you here. Taste you." He whispered the rest, and shock waves echoed deep inside her. She imagined his mouth there, felt him matching action to words.

How could something so hopelessly wrong feel this wonderful? Laine had told Murphy that the ability to inspire flaming passion wasn't one of her requirements for a mate. That had been such a short time ago, really. Before he'd introduced her to this euphoria, kindled responses so wanton that she didn't recognize herself. But like their surroundings, it wasn't real. It couldn't carry over once they'd left the mountains. Laine and Murphy were worlds apart, both geographically and in what they wanted. She wasn't the sort of woman who could indulge in a night of physical pleasure and then walk away in the morning with no regrets.

As readily as he'd sensed her unspoken desire moments ago, Murphy picked up on Laine's withdrawal. He tensed; his chest expanded with each harsh, rapid breath. At last his hands fell to his sides and he stepped back. Golden eyes held hers captive. "Not tonight." It was confirmation rather than question.

"Not ever," she whispered. Laine could hardly choke out those words of finality. Her throat hurt, her eyes stung. Doing the right thing shouldn't be so difficult. Murphy looked so downcast that she wanted to comfort him, relieve the palpable tension that emanated from him. But in doing so, she would be lost.

She edged around him and walked stiffly to the door. "I'm sorry, Murphy," she said without looking back, "but it can't be any other way. I'm looking for a husband, not a passionate fling."

Murphy's eyes narrowed as he watched the door click shut. Then he shook his head and a budding smile broke through the ferocious scowl. He scooped up the electric-blue scrap that she'd left behind. "Little coward. Don't you know it's already out of your hands?"

"SUNSHINE?"

Receiver in hand, Laine dropped her head back onto the bed. The noise she made was half moan, half yawn. Though his voice sounded deeper, more rugged than usual, she'd recognize the caller with her eyes closed. Which, now that she thought about it, was a terrific idea. Turning over she tucked the blanket up around her neck and cradled the phone to her ear with one shoulder.

"Laine? Is that you?"

"'M not sure." One eye opened to check the clock. Not yet eight. The last time she'd looked before falling asleep, it had read four thirty-nine. "Ask me in about four hours." His wide-awake chuckle annoyed her. *She* was supposed to be the morning person in this twosome. Both eyes shot open at that thought, and Laine struggled to sit up. It was a hard-won victory.

"What do you want, Murphy?" She didn't care that she sounded like him at his grumpiest.

"Hmm," he said, both amusement and satisfaction evident in his voice. "I've been wondering if all that cheerfulness ever wore thin."

"Of course it does. Until now you just hadn't pushed the right button."

"Not for lack of trying."

She shouldn't have answered the insistent ringing, Laine told herself. She wasn't up to fending off Murphy's ripostes after such a short night.

"What time are you leaving today?"

She blinked at his unexpected question. What was he up to now? "Sometime after noon, I suppose," she answered noncommittally, then couldn't contain the urge to ask, "Why?"

"I'd like to bum a ride if you're heading back to Atlanta."

Please, don't do this. She had spent too much of last night lamenting the fact that she wouldn't be seeing Murphy again. And in the wee hours she'd finally made the reluctant admission to herself. She wanted to be with him, to further explore the magnetism that pulled her to him. The chance to spend hours with him in the close confines of her car was so tempting. And so risky. Laine knew how vulnerable she was where Murphy was concerned. "It's a long drive."

She gave him credit for having a sound argument, built around the hassles of a van ride to Winston-Salem airport, then another plane change in Atlanta. But they were talking about something altogether different than the inconvenience of getting to Atlanta. They both knew it.

"Well," she hedged, "I have some business to take care of on the way. A stop down near the South Carolina border. I've no idea how long it will take." That ought to discourage him.

"No problem. I'm already packed, so just let me know when you're ready to go. See you in a while for Amanda's last meeting."

He hung up, making the decision for her. He might look and act indolent most of the time. But when Colin

Murphy wanted something, he didn't waste any time going after it.

Murphy's law.

After a final rousing session the group disbanded, all of them armed with a vigorous new approach to reaching their goals. Laine's original goal faded into oblivion when she saw Murphy's stowed luggage alongside hers in the Jeep. Even the smallest reminder of him was enough to distract her from everything else. She waved to Amanda as they backed out of a parking space, and the other woman responded with a thumbs-up good-luck signal. Laine knew she'd need more than luck. She had to be a masochist, sentencing herself to hours alone with Murphy. But she couldn't seem to help it.

"Dare I assume that your more conservative driving is a result of my subtle hints earlier in the week?"

"You can assume that, if you like," Laine told him blithely, as she turned on to the road at the end of the lodge's long, corrugated drive. "But you'd be deluding yourself. Now that we've hit pavement, we can fly."

"You mean it's white knuckle time again?"

She couldn't resist rising to the bait, even though she knew it was exactly what he wanted. "Traffic experts say that women can drive as well as men."

"Not only that, but they can do it on either side of the road."

"Murphy?"

"Yes, Sunshine?"

When Laine gave him a rather explicit order, he threw back his head and laughed. "Yes, Sunshine."

She smiled at his attempt to be meek and compliant, fully aware that Murphy was the least tractable male she'd ever met. "Why do you call me that?"

Out of the corner of her eye, Laine saw him shrug. "It just fits," he said casually, giving her the impression that he was evading the real reason for nicknaming her. She didn't push further. It was probably safer not to know.

A few miles farther along, Laine pointed out the dirt road that led to Boggy's place. She also confessed to slipping away the previous afternoon for another whittling lesson.

"Did you really find that old guy by taking a wrong turn on your way to the lodge?" Murphy asked. "It seems to me that you'd have to make a serious effort to stray from the main highway and end up back here."

"You know how confusing these mountain roads can be. I'll bet you couldn't drive straight to that remote lodge without at least one unplanned detour."

"You're probably right. I'm not much for car trips in general."

Laine resisted reminding him that he'd been quite persuasive about riding back to Atlanta with her. "You don't like to idle along on your way to somewhere, taking in the sights or stopping to talk to people as you go?"

"I never drive anywhere if I can avoid it. If we were meant to travel long distances by car, airplanes and helicopters wouldn't have been invented. Since they were, I take it as a sign that I'm supposed to use them."

"You miss a lot that way," she insisted, defending one of her favorite pastimes.

"Sure, like eyestrain, stiff legs, boredom and a numb backside. Give me a plane any day. At least it gets you where you're going in a hurry. I'm a man who likes his creature comforts."

Not for the first time, Laine wondered where Murphy lived. What sort of home would an architect choose for himself? She sensed he wasn't the New York or Chicago high-rise type. He'd mentioned that he liked being near the ocean, and she could see him living the Southern California life-style. But it was easier to picture him on a stretch of isolated, windswept beach farther up the coastline. Wherever his home was, he probably didn't spend much time there. Designing buildings all over the world must demand a lot of travel.

Before she'd started college, Laine's family had moved so many times that she lost count, and even then, her father had been gone more than he was with them. Her mother had endured it with capable stoicism, and Laine had learned to adjust. She'd battled early-childhood shyness, forcing herself to approach strangers and convert them into friends. But it hadn't been as easy for her twin sister. Maureen had hated the nomadic life-style, vowing that once she had a choice, she'd never live that way again. It was one dream they had shared for only a short period of time.

Of all the requirements for her ideal man, only one was nonnegotiable. She wouldn't even consider anyone whose job might be subject to constant travel and frequent transfers. Her future husband had to be stable and established in one place. A criterion that an itinerant architect definitely did not meet.

She shouldn't even be thinking about such things. Murphy wasn't suitable and she knew it. Why did she persist in trying to find qualities that weren't there? It was one thing to be curious about him, quite another to give the curiosity free rein. The less she knew about him, the safer she'd be. One would think that after repeating it all week, she'd be convinced by now.

Since weather was the most innocuous topic she could think of, Laine seized it. Inhaling deeply of the woodsy scent, she said, "I think your pal Andy is onto something. I've had a lot more energy since I started breathing this fresh, cool air. It's better than a vitamin pill. Does it affect you the same way?"

"I have low blood pressure. I never get very stirred up."

"Never?" Laine questioned with a raised eyebrow. Alluding to the previous night would only lead to more complications. He was silent for so long that she took her eyes off the road for a moment. Another mistake.

The man was a devil. All he had to do was remove his glasses and look at her—as he was doing right now—and her body turned hot enough to spark a forest fire. And, damn him, he knew it. Her reaction to him had always been painfully obvious.

"Well, almost never," he said, sending her a slow, sexy grin. "If the need . . . rises, I can bestir myself."

Couldn't he just? Laine had felt ample proof of that last night and was still experiencing aftershocks today.

For a man who was the antithesis of what she was looking for, Colin Murphy had a real talent for inciting her senses. She gripped the wheel tighter and made up her mind not to say another thing. Her resolve lasted at least a minute.

By midafternoon they'd pulled into a small town that boasted one traffic light and a business district that was only two blocks long. Laine stopped to ask directions and was told to follow the main street to the eastern outskirts and she couldn't miss it.

Sure enough, a large billboard arrow pointed the way to Darden's Textiles, a small locally owned company. She parked in a visitor's slot and retrieved a leather portfolio from behind her seat. Before going inside the modern plant, Laine took a cursory look at the abandoned one located about a hundred and fifty yards behind. There was another much smaller structure close to it, also in need of R&R's services. She suggested that Murphy wait for her in the reception area, and went in to meet Deke Darden.

Darden was a classic good old boy, the type Laine had frequently encountered during her seven years in business. She could almost predict what he would say. That made it easy to figure out how she would overcome his skepticism.

"Sit down, little lady," he boomed, shaking her outstretched hand after masking his surprise at her appearance. "I figured Laine was a man's name, you being in the demolition business, and all." He pronounced it *dee-moe-lition*.

"A common mistake," she assured him with a cheerful smile. Militant feminism never worked on these characters. You had to stay charming and affable. "People take one look at me and can't believe I could possibly know anything about blowing up buildings."

Darden cleared his throat, a sure sign she'd anticipated his next remark. He smoothed his tie down, but a good six inches of white shirt was still visible between the tip and his substantial waistline. "Um, well, I'm sure you know what you're doing, little lady, but—"

"You bet I do," she broke in, adjusting her accent and style of speech to sound more like his. "So let's you and me hike on out there to the site, and I'll tell you exactly what needs to be done to take care of your problem."

She was on her feet before he could voice an objection. By that time his ingrained Southern manners wouldn't allow him to do anything but follow her. All the while she was leading him out to the empty building, Laine recited details of similar projects R&R had done. She knew many of the names and locations would be familiar to him.

As they walked the boundaries of the old brick factory, Darden shook his fist at the banks of high windows. Most of them were now boarded up; a few were gaping holes rimmed by jagged glass, signs of recent damage. "Durn kids! First they tried using it for their beer busts. Then they took to vandalizing it bit by bit. Lord knows what's next. That's why I want to get rid of this eyesore before anything worse happens. Don't rightly feel secure about 'em messing around out here. Might take a notion to start in on my new plant."

"I understand," Laine said, launching immediately into a complicated explanation of the theory of implosion and how the job would be accomplished. She used plenty of technical jargon because, for some reason, people respected your competence more if they couldn't understand what you were talking about.

"And you can blow up this building that way? Without debris flying ever' which way?" Deke asked, scratching the balding spot on his crown. "Without damaging the new one?"

This was exactly where she wanted him. "I guarantee it. In fact, I'll be happy to give you a demonstration on the small building over there. Free of charge. I can make it collapse inward, so all that's left is a nice neat little pile of rubble that can be trucked away. All you have to do is sign an authorization form and go back to your office until the dust clears."

"Little lady, if you can do that, the job is yours."

Like most doubters, he was eager to give Laine the opportunity to fall flat on her face. But she could deliver on her promise, and Deke would have to eat his words. The job would be theirs. Deke had been an easier sell than most. She got his signature, and after nodding his understanding that the calculations and logistics would take a while, he lumbered off toward his office.

Laine walked back to the Jeep and got the equipment she'd need to carry out the job. Then she went to work. Doing what she did best.

SECONDS AFTER DETONATING her miniblasts, Laine watched dust and bricks and splintered wood settle within her carefully prescribed boundaries. She hadn't done any fieldwork for several years, but here was proof that she hadn't forgotten how to competently plan and execute a demolition project, however minor. Indeed, she'd had to be more precise than usual about the number of explosives required for such a small job, and where to place the charges. It was good to know she still had the touch.

The commotion had barely subsided when Laine heard footsteps pounding behind her. She glanced over her shoulder, surprised to see Murphy in a dead run.

"Are you all right?" He grabbed her upper arms and pulled her against him with so much force it nearly knocked the breath out of her. His whole body pulsed with agitation, his voice was harsh with a tension she'd never heard before.

"Of course I'm all right," she said, pulling back a fraction to study his face, pale beneath his tan. "Why wouldn't I be?"

Chest heaving, gulping air, he shook her several times, then seemed to realize what he was doing and jerked his hands away. "Dammit, you scared the life out of me. What the devil are you doing playing with dynamite? Didn't anyone ever teach you that stuff's dangerous?"

He stuffed both hands into his pockets, to keep from shaking her again, Laine figured. "I assure you, Murphy, that I never *play* with dynamite. I understand its composition and capabilities as well as the hazards.

Probably better than you do." She put more distance between them and removed her personalized white hard hat.

Instead of dispatching his anger, her confidence provoked it more. He snatched off his glasses and glowered furiously at her. "If you know so much about the risk, smart-mouth, what are you doing out here leveling buildings?"

"It's all in a day's work for us engineers," she shot back, baffled by Murphy's overreaction. For emphasis, her pink-polished index fingernail tapped the R&R logo on her protective headgear. "One of these *R*'s stands for Randolph, and demolition is our business."

He looked awestruck, as if he couldn't assimilate that bit of information into his perception of her. "You blow up things for a living?"

"We blow up big things," she confirmed smugly. "This was just an appetizer. We concentrate mostly on abandoned petrochemical plants and factories."

She had never heard so much disdain packed into one snort. Unfamiliar with this new, truly irate Murphy, Laine shook her finger teasingly at him. "Watch out, Murphy. You're raving."

"I am *not* raving. I never rave!" His careful enunciation implied his patience was being severely tested. He crammed the glasses back on, releasing her from his stormy gaze. "And I—dammit! Why are we arguing when I'm still shaking?"

His arms closed around her, and Laine felt proof of that in the fine tremors and accelerated pulse. His touch was more gentle than before, but no less insistent, and as seconds ticked by he seemed contented to simply hold her. As she stood in Murphy's embrace, the significance of what had just happened fell into place. He'd come running at a breakneck pace because he feared for her safety. Under other circumstances, from another man, Laine might have found such concern sweetly touching. From Colin Murphy it only reinforced that she was already too attached to him. Breaking free, she surveyed her handiwork rather than face the disturbing implications of his action.

A crowd was beginning to assemble and Laine could hear the jangle of Deke's massive key chain heralding his arrival. Turning back to Murphy, she said, "It shouldn't take much longer to wrap this up and we can be on our way. How about meeting me back at the Jeep?"

He nodded and left her with Deke, but she knew the discussion was only postponed. "What do you say, Mr. Darden? Do we have a deal?"

"A promise is a promise. You kept yours. I'll keep mine." They returned to his office to finalize the arrangements, and this time Deke offered his hand first. With that out of the way, Laine only had Murphy to face.

But all signs of his earlier outburst had vanished by the time she got to the wagon. Murphy didn't bring up his flare of temper and Laine was glad to let it drop. He did ask a number of questions about her career and seemed to find it perfectly reasonable for a woman to be in demolition. That pleased Laine until she asked herself why she needed his approval. Another disturbing implication.

With almost grim determination Laine set about restoring the light banter that felt so much safer than serious conversation with Murphy. When they stopped for gas just inside the Georgia state line, their amiable sparring had dissolved into easy conversation and laughter. From the very first, Laine had stubbornly refused to credit Murphy with even one of the qualities she was looking for in a man. But after spending concentrated time with him during the past week, she had to admit that he possessed not one, but several. Intelligence and a sense of humor counted for a lot in her book, and Murphy had an excess of both. It wasn't enough of course.

Self-sufficient men like him often viewed women as necessary for one thing only. He hadn't made any secret that he was ready and willing for them to become intimate. But he didn't strike her as the type who'd adjust to having the same woman around all the time. And as for children, the image of Murphy as a father was even more improbable than of him as a husband. Somehow neither dimmed his appeal.

She ought to be grateful that the seminar had ended when it did. Laine was realistic enough to know that proximity to Murphy was bound to lead to trouble, probably sooner rather than later. Look at what had happened in just a few days. With that in mind, she asked, "Shall I run you on out to the airport? What time is your flight?"

Murphy shifted in his seat, feigning interest in the lights of Atlanta's northern suburbs. "Uh, I don't have a flight tonight. I canceled it earlier today."

"Why?"

He could feel her eyeing him suspiciously. He didn't like being evasive, but there were times when it couldn't be avoided. "I decided that I'd take care of some business since I had to be here anyway." She'd lost some of her earlier wariness and he didn't want to reawaken it.

"Where will you stay?"

Her question zeroed in on the thing he'd been inwardly debating. If the choice were Murphy's, he would have said, "With you," but he thought better of it. That didn't divert him from trying to find out where she lived, though. "I don't want to put you to any trouble. Why don't you just go to your place and I'll call a cab from there."

"My house is fairly centrally located. It makes more sense for me to save you the trouble and expense of a cab. Sometimes it's a long wait at this time of night."

It was plain that she didn't want him on her home turf. Murphy could be tenacious when he wanted something, but tonight he was willing to give her some breathing space. Laine was too cautious for him to start closing in yet. He'd keep his Atlanta connection a secret for now. "I guess you can drop me at Colony Square, if you're sure it's not out of your way."

"No problem. It's practically on top of Ansley Park."

Interesting, he mused, congratulating himself on the subtlety of his detective work. She had a house, presumably in Ansley Park. That neighborhood was one of the most in-demand areas of the city. It appeared that the demolition business was very successful for Laine Randolph. Elaine, he reminded himself. As soon as he got hold of a phone book, he'd look up her address. If he couldn't find her that way, he could always contact her at R&R. Pursuing a woman like this was foreign to Murphy. Foreign and surprisingly exciting.

He told himself it was an encouraging sign that Laine seemed hesitant to say goodbye after she pulled up in front of the hotel.

"I...it's been fun," she said. "Take it easy...and, well, take care."

Murphy lifted his leather bag from the backseat and bent to give her an easy smile and a friendly wink. "See ya 'round."

5

LAINE TRANSFERRED the safety goggles to the top of her head and used her T-shirt sleeve to blot her damp face. It was only midmorning and already the cavernous R&R warehouse felt like a steam bath. The enervating heat made her think of the refreshing coolness of the mountains. Of Murphy.

She'd driven home last night after dropping him off, and promptly succumbed to an attack of melancholia. Normally she was relieved to get back to her cozy little bungalow after a trip. But this time it seemed to mock her with its quiet solitude. Instead of turning down the air conditioning she'd thrown open all the windows, needing the city sounds to prove that she wasn't really alone. But they hadn't dispelled the loneliness that hovered around her.

All her life, Laine had battled to keep the darker half of herself hidden. As she'd matured, the episodes of confidence-robbing bleakness occurred with decreasing frequency. Once she had her own home and business, Laine thought she had mastered the problem for good. After her sister Maureen's sad example, she'd worked doubly hard to avoid giving in to any form of depression.

Yet something as simple as realizing she'd seen the last of Colin Murphy plunged her into depths that not even twelve hours of sleep could drive away. Laine had got up this morning torn between wishing she'd never met Murphy and wishing he was there the minute she opened her eyes.

She had gone to North Carolina as spontaneously as she did most everything else. But to be honest, she hadn't expected to find a husband. So why did coming home to her real life seem like a letdown?

Because, while watching Murphy walk away the night before, she had finally admitted that she didn't want him to go. He didn't fit her ideal-man profile. He wouldn't offer her the kind of future she needed, hadn't been interested enough in her to mount a full-scale pursuit. Oh, he'd have indulged in a no-strings-attached vacation affair if she'd been receptive, but he hadn't been crushed when it didn't develop. And he hadn't even looked back after figuratively kissing her off with his cavalier farewell. This morning Laine knew why none of those factors mattered. She was emotionally involved with Murphy.

For more than two years, she had shied away from relationships that demanded entrusting her feelings to another. But she hadn't forgotten the signs.

At this point there wasn't much she could do about the attachment, except hope it didn't last too long. Murphy was gone—she didn't know where. He hadn't asked for her phone number, and as a protective measure, she had scrupulously avoided any personal inquiries about him. Now it was too late. He was out of her life for good.

"Ah, the huntress returns," a deep voice thundered from behind her. "What's this? No husband?" He looked all around, as if he expected the man in question to be lurking in the shadowy corners of the warehouse. "Why, I can't believe it."

Laine smiled a greeting. She was used to Randy Williamson's droll gibes. "Why don't I just say you were right and we can bypass the rest of this exchange?" Blunt and blustery, her partner had informed her that she wouldn't find what she was looking for in the mountains. Just the opposite of what Murphy's friend Andy had predicted. Why must everything remind her of that insidious man?

"You're supposed to be on vacation. I didn't expect to see you here first thing this morning."

"You knew I was coming back to work on the raft." She surveyed the half-completed project. "What do you think of my innovative design?"

"Hmm," Randy said, walking the length of a flatbed trailer. "It lacks the imaginative absurdity of some of our *Wreck Tech* parade entries." He slapped one of the brushed-silver pontoons with his huge hand, nodding when he heard the hollow metallic hum. "But it ought to float, which is the primary consideration."

"Float!" Laine protested indignantly, hands on her hips. "You are looking at the future winner of the Ramblin' Regatta." The Great Chattahoochee Raft Race had been outlawed several years earlier when it grew too big and too rowdy. Too many participants took the event too seriously, and there had been numerous mishaps and injuries. Since then, a group of diehards had come up with their own by-invitation-only challenge. The new version consisted mostly of engineers who took pride in dreaming up some of the most bizarre craft ever to float.

"I don't know, Laine," Randy said, cocking one eyebrow skeptically. "So far, it looks like the remains from one hell of a party."

"Only someone lacking discrimination would look at this masterpiece and see two dozen aluminum beer kegs welded together. But wait until you see my secret weapon. I plan to keep it under wraps until the last minute so word doesn't leak out to our opposition. The crew is lined up to put the finishing touches on it Friday night. We'll start about six, and afterward I'm having pizza delivered."

Randy cleared his throat. "That's what I came to talk to you about. Hudson's overseeing that reassembly project in Mexico, but he got knocked out of commission by a virus. I'm flying down there tonight to fill in for him."

Raft race forgotten, Laine asked, "Is there anything you need me to take over for you on this end? My vacation plans are flexible, and I'll be in town all week anyway."

"Everything is under control. I should be back in less than a week. But you'd better find someone to fill in for me in the race."

Laine rubbed the bridge of her nose, taking a mental inventory of their employees. "I suppose I could draft someone from the office staff." Reviewing the possibilities, she frowned. "A muscle man would be better, but all our crews are out on jobs now."

"*I'm* available."

Standing just inside the open warehouse bay, he was a dark silhouette against the sun at his back. But his voice was unmistakable. "Murphy!" Laine exclaimed, hurrying toward him. "I thought— What are you— Oh, damn!"

"That's quite a greeting, Sunshine. Not quite up to your usual articulate standards, but I get the message."

"My mouth couldn't catch up with my brain," Laine said, laughing self-consciously. "You're about the last person in the world I expected to see today."

"Why should you be surprised? Last night I said I'd be seeing you."

"I thought you were speaking in general terms." Several strands had escaped from her messy ponytail, and he tucked one of them behind her ear. It was a simple gesture that meant nothing. Laine felt the intimacy of it all the way to the soles of her feet.

"You should know me well enough by now to realize that I never speak in generalities. I'm always very specific about what I say. And what I want."

Laine nodded. Far from being over, her relationship with Murphy was only beginning. Her instincts had tried to tell her that, but she'd been bent on denying the inevitable. All her resistance had been wearing, to say nothing of nonproductive.

Laine's birthday was in less than two weeks; her goal of finding a husband was surely further away than that.

Since the goal was unattainable by her deadline, Laine decided to postpone her hunt for a while longer. Murphy was with her now and it felt just right. It might not lead anywhere, but at least she'd enjoy herself. She was free for the next three weeks. What were vacations for, if not to be a little daring?

Amanda's warning about rationalizing echoed inside her head. "We all do what we want to do—and make excuses for the rest." Well, Laine thought rashly, everyone was entitled to a good rationalization every now and then.

She grinned, suddenly elated. "Come meet my partner and see what I'm working on." She performed introductions; the two men shook hands and Randy excused himself to get ready for his trip to Mexico.

"He's a big one, isn't he?" Murphy commented after Randy left.

"Six-five, I think, though his bearish build and that wild cinnamon-colored beard make him look even more imposing. The booming voice only enhances his ferocious image. Beneath it all he's a giant cream puff, but his friends allow him to preserve the illusion."

"How close a friend are you?"

Caught off guard, Laine gave him a quick glance. He was examining the welds that held two kegs together as if fascinated by the raft's construction. But she was sure he hadn't asked about Randy out of idle curiosity. Underlying the question, she detected a hint of jealousy and possibly latent possessiveness, elements she would never have associated with Murphy.

"Close like friends who've known each other for over ten years. And close like people are when they've been business partners since college graduation." She paused so her next statement would have the desired impact. "But not close like lovers. Ever." She raised both brows. "Does that tell you what you need to know?"

Laine assumed that he aimed for his smile to look contrite, but if so, he failed miserably. "Murphy, I don't think humility is your long suit. Next time you want to know something, just ask straight out."

"Will you give me straight answers?"

"No promises. You'll just have to ask and see." She aimed a playful poke at his biceps. "Now if you're serious about volunteering your services Saturday—or maybe I'm jumping the gun. Are you going to stay in Atlanta that long? Do you really want to do this?"

His look was daunting, an eloquent reminder that he usually said and did only what suited him. Apart from scavenging garbage, playing golf and taking a dip fully clothed, Laine remembered. Which added up to the conclusion that she exerted as dramatic an influence on Murphy as he did on her. Somehow that was reassuring.

"Consider yourself drafted. Now I need to give you a crash course in river rafting."

She spent the rest of the morning explaining how the superstructure of her raft would be mounted over twin pontoons, their concern for stability versus maneuverability, the difficulty in locating lightweight balsa wood. Since Murphy seemed genuinely interested and asked a number of pertinent questions, she even revealed the details of her brainstorm that she planned to unveil Friday night. "I think that will give us the edge we need to win. How does it sound to you?"

"Like a far-fetched Rube Goldberg invention. Are you sure it wouldn't be just as efficient to give canoe paddles to those two people in the middle?"

"It might work as well, but then our entry would look the same as all the others." She held a fabricated aluminum cone to the front of one of the pontoons, testing it for fit. "I don't want to just win. I want to do it with panache."

Murphy laughed. "I don't know if this will come in first, but it's a cinch it will get people's attention."

Laine's watch issued a string of strident beeps and she saw him frown.

"You have an appointment?"

"Later this afternoon. But I wanted to allow enough time to eat and digest." She picked up a handful of tools and carried them to a workbench.

"Uh-oh. Another foray into the great outdoors. What is it this time?" His voice was full of tolerant humor.

"Tennis," she replied, letting him have his fun. "You're safe. I'm meeting three friends at the club for doubles."

"A country club?" Scorn replaced his amusement.

"It's only a few blocks from my house, which makes it the closest place for golf, tennis and swimming. Not that I need an excuse for belonging to a place where I can have fun and get exercise." One of her pet peeves was people who insisted they didn't have to defend their actions, then did it anyway. As she'd just done. "You have something against country clubs?" She sounded almost as belligerent as Murphy.

"Not really. In fact, they provide reasonably harmless sanctuaries for a bunch of people that I might have to associate with otherwise."

Laine burst out laughing. "Murphy, I think you're a big fraud. But to prove that I don't hold it against you, I'll treat you to lunch at the best place to eat in Atlanta. Are you ready to go?"

"It's casual?" he asked, making her aware for the first time of the brevity of her outfit. Her khaki shorts were just that—short, revealing a wealth of skin between the cuffs and her shocking pink sneakers. The white Georgia Tech Yellowjacket T-shirt covered her well enough. But it was thin from years of wear and she didn't have on anything underneath it, which would be apparent to anyone who paid attention to such things. Murphy was paying attention.

She grabbed up some more tools to keep from crossing her arms over her breasts. It was silly to be prudish about territory he'd already covered with his hands. "No, we won't have any problem getting served." He had on a pair of white painter's pants, another of his omnipresent Hawaiian shirts and sockless deck shoes. Laine wondered what kind of business he'd conducted dressed like that. She supposed that eccentric creative geniuses could get by with wearing whatever they wanted. Who would object? She stashed the drill and wrenches in their assigned slots, then washed her hands at a deep sink. "Are you game?"

He shrugged and took his turn at the sink. "Eating at your favorite place is bound to be a piece of cake compared to some of your other adventures. Lead on."

Laine bypassed the company Wagoneer that she'd driven to the mountains. She pushed a button to lower the large overhead door and walked to a dark moss-green Stingray parked nearby. Murphy gave the car a thorough once-over before climbing into the passenger seat. "Old, but fast. Right?"

"You got it. It's hard to find four hundred and twenty-seven inches of cubic displacement nowadays." To underscore her point, she revved up the powerful engine and peeled out of the parking lot. After fifteen minutes of deftly negotiating congested noontime traffic, Laine turned off North Avenue into a crowded multistoried parking lot.

"This is it? The Varsity is your favorite place to eat in the whole city?"

"If I don't eat here at least once a week, I have withdrawal symptoms." She whipped into a space that had just been vacated. "Besides, I love to eat in the car. Makes me nostalgic for the old days, I guess. Like *American Graffiti*."

"I don't think you're old enough to be nostalgic for the early sixties," he said dryly. "You were barely out of diapers then."

"Come on, Murphy. You're not exactly Father Time. How old are you, anyway?"

It was the first truly personal question she'd asked him and Murphy felt like doing a tap dance in the parking lot. Instead he answered matter-of-factly, "I'll be thirty-seven in November."

Penetrating was the only way to describe the way she looked at him. "Of course. You're a Scorpio. I should have guessed."

"Why?"

"Your eyes. Scorpio eyes are usually a giveaway. I overlooked the obvious because I was so sure you were a crab. No offense." She turned to smile at the carhop and rattled off an order without consulting Murphy. He heard "dogs all the way, fries, rings, peach pies, frosted orange." He didn't think the car was big enough to hold all that food, and when the tray was attached to the window, he was sure he couldn't eat that much.

As she usually did when she wanted him to try something new, Laine turned bossy, like a school-teacher lecturing her reluctant pupil. But rather than causing Murphy to condemn her as just another med-dlesome female, this trait made her more endearing to him. In fact, he wanted her to keep right on interfering in his life. Picking up a flimsy paper plate, he told him-self he must be going crazy. At that precise moment, as he bit into an onion-laden chili dog, Murphy knew.

It wasn't insanity. It was love. Or at least the begin-ning of it. He almost choked.

If he'd expected it to happen to him—and he hadn't— he would never have anticipated that the bolt would hit while he stuffed down greasy fast food in a cramped car. It shouldn't surprise him. Laine had been different right from the start.

"Here, have a drink of this frosted orange," she suggested, handing him a red cup. "It'll make everything settle easier."

He took several swallows. "Everything is settling just fine, Sunshine." She gave him an odd look, most likely because he sounded slightly shell-shocked. He could also feel a goofy smile spreading over his face, one that probably resembled Andy's at its most saccharine. Murphy could see that this love business was going to take some getting used to. Good thing he had plenty of time to devote to the project.

He had no trouble convincing Laine to invite him to her club late that afternoon. It made perfect sense for him to swim while she and her friends played tennis. After they showered and dressed, the only logical thing to do was have drinks on the patio and dinner on the glassed-in porch.

Every day that week he managed to occupy the lion's share of her time. It was easy, as it had been at first in the mountains before she backed off from their powerful physical attraction. Murphy took pains not to push that aspect of their relationship, confident that it would evolve naturally as she got to know him in other ways.

Part of each day was spent working on the raft. But there was still time for long walks in Piedmont Park, which was near her house, and early one morning, they climbed Stone Mountain. They rode the Marta subway from its farthest northern point to the airport, just because Laine said it was a fun way to watch people. One afternoon, when Murphy insisted it was too hot and sticky to be anywhere other than a cool, dark theater, they sat through three movies in a row. They shared picnic lunches and elegant dinners. And every night he went back to a solitary room after leaving Laine with a chaste kiss. Forbearance was an admirable trait. He was sure of it. But a little went a long way.

Friday evening after the raft was pronounced raceworthy and the pizza devoured, Laine dropped Murphy off at his hotel saying she would pick him up the next morning. Then she left him with one final instruction. Watching the Corvette roar away, he was torn between cautioning himself not to get his hopes up and shouting, "Hot damn!"

She'd said, "Bring some extra clothes so you can shower and change at my house when we get back from the river."

RACE TIME WAS TEN O'CLOCK, but R&R had its entry in the water by nine. It was a curious-looking affair, with slats of balsa wood spanning the framework, which perched atop twin beer-keg pontoons. In the center, two lightweight racing bicycles were mounted front to back over open wells. Half a dozen crew members, looking rustic in cutoffs with suspenders, plaid shirts and straw hats, ridiculed the competition as unimaginative and slow.

Laine smiled at the requisite clowning while she made a last minute adjustment to the pulleys attached to the bike chains. She had chosen this group as much for their love of fun and challenge as for their strength. When a crowd began to congregate on the bank, she said, "I knew my revolutionary raft design would turn heads."

"Most of them couldn't care less about this pile of kegs and boards. It's your bodily design that fascinates them," Murphy muttered.

His bold gaze wandered over her denim shorts, lingering a few seconds on the shirt that was knotted above her bare midriff.

"Speak for yourself." Her teasing retort sounded more like a breathless dare.

"I am, Sunshine."

Had any other man looked at her that way, Laine would accuse him of leering. But when Murphy caressed her with those avid eyes, her stomach went into a free-fall. All week long she'd been puzzled by his cooled ardor. Today, it was back in full force. The question was what she would do with it.

"Hey, Laine," a man from another raft yelled. "We're supposed to use paddle power, not pedal. It's an unwritten rule. Guess you're disqualified. Too bad."

"Got you on a technicality, Ron," she called back, rapping one set of handlebars. "This is just another way to generate extra paddle power." She treated him to a complex explanation of how the bike chains attached to pulleys, which turned the smaller versions of old-fashioned paddlewheels. "You guys might as well quit now. Shot down by superior design and craftsmanship."

They baited each other for several more exchanges, then it was time to settle down and race. Laine made sure everyone buckled on a life jacket because, although the Chattahoochee wasn't too deep, it was crooked, and the current was swift. Contenders lined up two abreast so officials could green flag them off at one-minute intervals to avoid congestion at the starting line. After that it was every team for itself. The R&R crew was in the fourth wave to cast off, quickly pulling ahead of the neighboring raft and closing in on the slower of the pair that left right before them. The four remaining craft had already disappeared around the first bend in the river.

"One at a time," Laine instructed, acting as cheerleader. "Catch up with this one first, then worry about the next." Sitting astride the front bike gave her a better perspective than that of the three paddlers on each side. From her position she plotted and directed strategy, deciding when to hold steady for a turn and when to approach it full speed.

They had covered about half the racecourse when her legs began to tire. Keeping up the steady, brisk pace was difficult so she asked to trade places with one of the paddlers. She ended up behind Murphy, who was handling his substitute role with quiet efficiency. He hadn't once described this project as lunacy, as she'd have expected. Every day he had worked alongside her without complaint, as he was doing now. Laine watched him dip the aluminum paddle into murky red-brown water with smooth, measured strokes, even giving his wrist the proper flick before lifting the paddle for another stroke. It was a repetitive, rhythmic motion that stirred her in a purely sensual way. Get your mind on the race, she told herself, moving a little faster to compensate for her lapse.

By the time they entered the last half mile, only one raft was ahead of them. "It's Bainbridge and his gang. Are we going to let that bunch of slugs beat us again this year?" Laine urged.

A chorus of "Hell, no," rang out as they braced for the final onslaught. Battling furiously they pulled even, fell behind, then surged in front by a hair, only to be overtaken again. The teamwork of gliding, coordinated strokes gave way to frenzied pumping, each individual digging into reserves of strength for one last burst of speed. The raft bucked like a crazed stallion, sending dirty water foaming up around them and making it nearly impossible to stay aboard.

Surrounded by almost deafening noise, the two contenders crossed the finish line neck and neck, then slowed and altered course for the bank where the judges waited. Both teams confidently claimed victory, but no winner could be declared until all entries finished and official times were calculated.

Along with their teammates, Murphy and Laine scrambled onto shore, trying to recover land legs after the wild ride. A boisterous group of friends who had come to cheer them on insisted the raft should take a victory lap, which meant putting it on the trailer and hauling it back to the embarkation point.

"You can make as many trips as you want," Laine said, pulling a towel out of her tote, which had been left downriver with her car before the race started. She wiped her face and arms before handing the towel to Murphy with a smile. "But we have other plans."

His startled look said, "We do?" but Laine wasn't divulging any more.

"We'll help you trailer it and then you're on your own," she added.

She searched for her keys while watching them hoist the cumbersome craft and maneuver it onto the flatbed. Then, because most of the crew was young and prone to horseplay, one of them charged another, using his paddle as a combination lance and sword.

That was all the encouragement needed for a full-scale battle to erupt. Metal clanged as they wielded the lightweight aluminum with more strength and enthusiasm than skill. Laine laughed as one combatant gave a victory cry and with a crashing blow sent his opponent's weapon flying. But Murphy picked that exact second to step from behind the raft.

The airborne paddle struck the bone on his wrist with a dull thunk and fell to the ground. The only sound Murphy made was a whoosh of expelled breath.

"Oh, no!" Laine cried, dropping the tote to rush forward. Murphy looked a bit shocked and he hadn't moved. "Lord, how bad is it?" The injury wasn't visible, but she knew it must be painful. She herded him toward a plastic lawn chair one of the spectators had been sitting in.

"It's not that bad," he insisted, but she could tell that the bravado was uttered through gritted teeth.

"Don't try to be brave, Murphy. I know it has to hurt. Here, sit down." She gently pushed him into the chair. "Now stay put and I'll be back in a flash."

Within seconds she had captured the ubiquitous tote and rushed back to his side. Gingerly she probed his wrist. "Oh, dear. I'm totally inept at first aid. I'll ask around. Maybe there's a doctor or nurse in the crowd."

"Laine, calm down," he said, pushing her hand away. "And please stop fussing."

"But it's all my fault that you're even here."

"Oh, brother. I can't believe you're having a guilt trip over such a little thing."

"Little thing! You're probably going to need a cast." She massaged her own arm in sympathy. "X rays. That's what you need. Can you walk to the car?"

Murphy gave a mighty sigh, but his voice sounded authoritative. "Sunshine, trust me. I don't need a cast, or X rays. It's no big deal. And, yes, I can walk." He started to get up, using his wrist as a lever. At his slight wince, Laine protested. "It hurts some, okay? But I'll live."

Laine was on her hands and knees, dragging an incredible assortment of paraphernalia out of the tote, talking to herself. "I saw it only last week. It has to be in here somewhere."

"Everything is in there somewhere."

"I know your sarcasm is a cover-up because you're in extreme pain," she said soothingly. She continued to dig until she came up with a box containing an elastic bandage. "This should make it better."

Her concern was so earnestly appealing that Murphy was almost glad the incident had happened. Tolerable pain wasn't a bad trade for Laine's tender mercies. She made a cute mother hen. Contrary to what he'd said, he found her fussing over him both engaging and encouraging. But he'd rather she did it in private instead of in front of their growing audience. "Uh, Sunshine, I'm beginning to feel like the main attraction. Do you think we could just leave and forget the bandage?"

She bit her lip as if he'd requested her to make a life-and-death decision. "I guess it won't make that much difference. I'll get you to the emergency room as fast as I can."

He stood up abruptly. "You can get me to your house—not a hospital—as fast as you can. After that, I will take a shower, put on the clean clothes you told me to bring, and then we will spend the remainder of the day as planned. All right?"

"Oh, all right," she grumbled, muttering something about him issuing orders like Smokin' Joe. "Come on."

He suspected her capitulation was temporary and he was right. She argued all the way back into the city, but once Murphy made up his mind about something, he was unwavering. He would stand for a little bit of fussing, but the one thing he didn't need was Laine feeling maternal toward him. He had a different sort of attention in mind.

Now, standing in her bathroom, drying himself with one of her plush yellow towels, surrounded by the soft scents of femininity, Murphy was acutely aware of how desperately he wanted Laine. She hadn't just gotten under his skin—she'd seeped into his soul. A couple of weeks ago he couldn't picture any female invading his life. Today he couldn't imagine a future without Sunshine. He shook his head and draped the towel over a porcelain rack. No question about it. He'd fallen victim to terminal sappiness.

He picked up a tiny, expensive-looking fluted bottle, lifted the stopper and inhaled. Like the woman who wore it, the perfume was sweet, subtle and sexy as hell. Painfully so, he thought, reaching for his clean clothes. As soon as they'd arrived, Laine had ushered him through her bedroom and into the bath. Despite assurances that a blow on the wrist didn't prevent him from climbing stairs, she'd insisted on using the guest shower herself. At the moment, he wasn't sure she'd done him any favors.

A light tap on the door preceded her question. "Murphy? Are you about ready?"

"If you only knew," he said under his breath while struggling with his zipper.

"I've just the thing to make you forget your pain."

"Tell me about it." He took a couple of deep breaths and reached for the doorknob. "Coming." Murphy grimaced at his choice of words.

"You look better," Laine said, her frown diminishing a bit when she saw him. "How do you feel now?"

He might feel better if she didn't look so tempting in those white shorts and loosely belted matching shirt. With her hair bound by a yellow ribbon and her feet bare, Laine looked as fresh and natural as she had the day he first saw her. Murphy admitted he'd wanted her right from the beginning. But it was nothing compared to the way he felt now. "As I've been trying to tell you for the past hour, I'm fine." His voice sounded as tightly wound as the rest of his body felt.

"Men!" she said, making it sound like an indictment. She tugged him toward her bed. "Why do you have to act like such tough guys when you're sick or hurt? Well, never mind. I know how to take care of that." She whipped back the dark green floral coverlet, revealing creamy yellow sheets that matched the walls.

"No arguments. You lie down and I'll be back to take care of you in just a minute."

6

MURPHY WAS FRANKLY CONFUSED. While she clearly intended to install him in her bed, she was going about it in a briskly efficient manner that had nothing to do with seduction. He could almost visualize Laine tucking him in, then dusting her hands and abandoning him.

"You get settled while I fix us a snack, and when I get back we'll watch a movie." She opened one of the double closet doors and took a fluffy down comforter from the top shelf. "But first, wrap this around you."

The shorts stretched with her and Murphy got a glimpse of even more leg. He did *not* need anything to make him hotter. "Laine, it's eighty-seven degrees outside."

"I can fix that." She flipped the thermostat as far down as it would go. "In a few minutes, it'll be fifty-five."

He studied her and the comforter she'd handed him. "Bear with me if I seem dense, but why make it frigid in here so I can bundle up in covers?"

She looked at him as if he had suddenly gone witless, but quickly followed up with a tolerant smile. She must have decided that the accident had impaired his thought processes. "Trust me, Murphy. When you don't feel well, you just have to give in to it and indulge yourself. The best way to do that is to watch an old movie and munch on something good. But you have to huddle under a blanket or it doesn't work."

He was beginning to see the possibilities. "In bed."

Laine opened an armoire that contained a television and video recorder. "A couch will work equally well. It just happens that my VCR is in the bedroom." She inserted a tape and punched some buttons. "Stop stalling and crawl in. I won't be gone long."

Murphy dropped the comforter on the bed and followed her into the kitchen. He leaned against the door frame and watched her put something in the microwave to defrost, then set about measuring popcorn and butter into an electric popper. Over her shoulder, Laine spotted him and shook her head in a gesture of disapproval. "You're not doing well with your orders."

Ignoring that, he followed her to the refrigerator, propping his elbows on the open door. The only things on the top shelf were two bottles placed on their sides, and a gallon-jar of dills. "Hmm, champagne and pickles. Do we have them together?"

"Of course not." She shuddered. "I love both, but I don't think the flavors are complementary. We'll stick with the dills today."

"And the champagne?" he asked, carrying the heavy jar to the counter.

"I always keep a supply on hand. You never know when you might have something to celebrate." Laine got a bed tray out of the pantry and put a colorful place mat and matching napkins on it. "You're supposed to be resting," she scolded, fixing him with a stern glare. "Too bad you don't have some pajamas to put on. Wearing them helps you feel even more pampered."

When he gave her a skeptical look, she said, "Scratch that. You're probably not the type." She waved her hand dismissively. "Whatever, go back in there and make yourself comfortable. I'll be along shortly and I expect to see you bundled up in that comforter. Now, shoo!"

Murphy made his way back through the dining and living rooms of the small house, his grin threatening to become a full-blown laugh. She'd insisted. He couldn't be blamed for following orders.

Laine dumped the buttered popcorn into a bowl, arranged four enormous dill pickles on a salad plate, added a saucer piled high with her homemade fudge and fixed two large glasses of Coke. This wasn't how she'd foreseen spending the afternoon, but fun came in different forms. She had enjoyed everything she and Murphy had done so far. Playing couch potato would be just one more adventure. With a flourish she swept up her goodies and headed for the bedroom.

"Here we go." She braced one knee on the bed and deposited the overflowing tray in the middle. Before settling down, she retrieved some extra pillows and plumped several behind Murphy's back. His bare back. He must have taken off his shirt because, although he had gotten under the covers, the room was still very warm. Laine smiled at his surprising compliance with her instructions. "Ready at last," she announced, depressing the remote-control button to start the tape.

NO COST! NO OBLIGATION TO BUY!
NO PURCHASE NECESSARY!

PLAY "LUCKY 7"
AND GET AS MANY AS SIX FREE GIFTS...

HOW TO PLAY:

1. With a coin, carefully scratch off the silver box at the right. This makes you eligible to receive one or more free books, and possibly other gifts, depending on what is revealed beneath the scatch-off area.

2. You'll receive brand-new Temptation® novels. When you return this card, we'll send you the books and gifts you qualify for absolutely free!

3. Unless you tell us otherwise, every month we'll send you 4 additional novels to read and enjoy. If you decide to keep them, you'll pay only $2.24 per book*, a savings of 26¢ per book. There is no extra charge for postage and handling. There are no hidden extras.

4. When you join Harlequin Reader Service, we'll send you additional free gifts from time to time, as well as our newsletter.

5. You must be completely satisfied. You may cancel at any time just by dropping us a line or returning a shipment of books at our cost.

* Terms and prices subject to change.

DETACH AND MAIL CARD TODAY

BUSINESS REPLY CARD

First Class   Permit No. 717   Buffalo, NY

Postage will be paid by addressee

Harlequin Reader Service®
901 Fuhrmann Blvd.,
P.O. Box 1867
Buffalo, NY 14240-9952

NO POSTAGE
NECESSARY
IF MAILED
IN THE
UNITED STATES

After the opening credits, dramatic strains of piano and orchestra music faded into a scene of London on a rainy night. Murphy reached for a handful of popcorn and asked, "You like Ingrid Bergman?"

"Mmm," Laine affirmed, savoring a bite of fudge as it dissolved on her tongue. "But I like Cary Grant even better. *Indiscreet* is my absolute favorite movie of all time. I'm a sucker for fifties' romantic comedies."

They munched in companionable silence for a few minutes until the Bergman character was chastised by her sister for expecting too much from a man when she wanted him to be able to talk a little. In the sister's opinion, there was a limit to how entertaining men can be. If he was good-looking and danced beautifully, that's all a woman was entitled to.

"You agree with that, Sunshine? Are handsomeness and social graces really that important to women? Are they enough?"

Laine couldn't imagine Murphy being insecure because he lacked classic good looks. And he could have tempered his gruff bluntness if he cared about social graces, which he obviously didn't. But that didn't explain the nuance she'd heard beneath the nonchalance of his question. She couldn't explain why, but she needed to reassure him.

"I don't object to a man being handsome, or suave, or sophisticated. The idea of Cary Grant across the breakfast table boggles my mind. But a lot of men who look great act as if that gives them special dispensation to be irresponsible skunks. Or worse, boring." She weighed her next words carefully. "Bergman's character, Anna, is right. Looks are unimportant if a man has something interesting to say." *As you always do.*

Murphy regarded her seriously for a moment longer, then grinned. She wondered if he'd read her thoughts. He crunched into a pickle. "You know, this weird combination of food tastes pretty good. I like it."

Laine smiled, inordinately pleased. "I'm glad. As I said, all this is designed to take your mind off the pain."

"You wanna play doctor?"

She laughed delightedly and gave him a chastening rap on the arm. "Behave, Murphy. Be a good patient or I'll take away your treats." As Laine could have predicted, he didn't look the least bit remorseful.

The story unfolded with Grant deceiving Bergman by pretending to be a married man who could never get a divorce. In reality, he was a happy bachelor who never wanted to get married. The subterfuge was a form of protection, his way of warning off women whose aim was matrimony. If a woman knew the score up front and was still interested in him, then the decision—and responsibility for it—was hers. In his mind, he was behaving honorably. Bergman, swept off her feet by the rogue's charm, swallowed her pride and decided to ignore his marital status and have a romantic fling with him.

"How about *that*?" Murphy asked, selecting the biggest remaining piece of fudge. "How would you feel if the man you were...involved with deceived you? Pretended to be something he wasn't?"

Laine swallowed against an inexplicable tightness in her chest and forced herself to look at him. As before, she knew he had a personal motivation for asking that particular question. Surely he wasn't— No, Murphy had told her he wasn't married and she believed him. He was too straightforward to lie about something that important. So what had he done, or said, that wasn't on the level?

"I suppose in real life that sort of deception would be devastating. But in the make-believe world of movies, it's easy to see why a woman would forgive Cary Grant almost anything. His charm is a killer. And it's so effortless."

Murphy grunted his reluctant agreement. "You mean like later on in the movie when the brother-in-law says he believes that success with women is something you're born with, and you don't deserve any of the credit?"

"You've already seen this?" Laine exclaimed.

He shrugged. "What can I say? I'm a sucker for fifties' romantic comedies, too. Guess I shouldn't admit that, huh? Men are supposed to go in for adventure and war. Violence." He lifted one exposed shoulder again. "Me, I like anything that has heaven and angels and ghosts. Or musicals, especially the funny, silly ones. And Ingrid Bergman."

"Then I'm glad I chose *Indiscreet.*" She burrowed beneath the comforter before stopping to think that Murphy might see it as something other than an attempt to escape the cold. But he was engrossed in the screen so Laine relaxed to watch the rest of the movie.

Murphy transferred the tray to the floor when the popcorn was gone. Laine thought he inched a little closer to the middle of the bed when he resettled himself, but she couldn't be sure. Not that she cared. She was feeling mellow and, to be honest, receptive. Murphy had been a perfect gentleman all week, but she had missed his inflaming kisses.

By the time Ingrid Bergman was bemoaning that she and Cary Grant were fated not to be married, Murphy's arm was around Laine and her head rested on his shoulder. They hadn't been calculated moves, but rather logical extensions of the movie's romantic ambience and the secluded intimacy surrounding them.

During the closing scene, when the tables are turned and it is Grant who insists that Bergman will like being married to him, Laine slid her hand onto Murphy's chest. He covered it, holding it in place while his thumb drifted lazily over her fingers.

Laine was hypnotized by the sensual cadence of his stroking. She felt it all over, not just where his hand touched hers. It took several seconds after the movie ended and the tape went snowy before she remembered that it had to be shut off. She sat upright, scrambling to locate the remote control, but he was ahead of her. He leaned across her to the edge of the bed and punched the right button. Suddenly it was very quiet. And he was very close. Laine wondered if that realization inspired in Murphy the same longings that she was feeling. It didn't take long to find out.

Kisses fell on her face, delicate as snowflakes but infinitely warmer. After a timeless interlude his mouth lingered longer, became bolder, and the warmth deepened.

Excitement, dormant for the past week, flared to life when their lips fused and his tongue dipped inside her mouth to take his fill of her moist softness. Laine's breath escaped on a broken moan because the magic went on and on, awakening, building.

"A week, Laine," he murmured huskily. "Too long. I've been hungry for the taste of you. I couldn't have waited much longer."

"I know," she whispered, tracing his jawline with her forefinger. "Taste some more."

His lips pressed down to take hers again, the momentum easing Laine onto her back. She welcomed the fierce heat of his kiss as she yielded to his weight. She shifted restlessly, need mounting with every quick, hard thrust of his tongue until she cried out, "Murphy!"

He drew back and the golden heat of his eyes sent sensual tremors cascading through her. "Tasting's not enough."

"No," she breathed, willing him to touch her, gasping when he did.

Perhaps being an architect gave him an understanding, an appreciation for texture and form. His hands, gentle and sensitive, glided slowly over every delicate curve and graceful swell, as if intent on committing each one to memory. In delicious concert, his lips paid homage to her shoulders, her neck, her face.

He licked the tender spot behind her ear, then whispered what her shudders did to him. Laine silently implored him to prove it.

"You're allowed to touch too, Sunshine."

She started, shocked that she'd been lying passive, her hands at her sides like dead weights. In her mind, she'd caressed every inch of him, felt the arousing contrast between the satiny skin of his back, the prickly coarseness of his beard, the velvety hardness that signaled the intensity of his desire for her. Her fingers went to his face and she was rewarded by his groan of satisfaction.

Her hands swept over his back, trailed lower. Lower. "Murphy! You don't have any clothes on."

"Uh, oh. You noticed."

"Did you think I wouldn't?" The glint in his eyes contradicted any innocence he might claim. "It's not easy to disguise an omission like that."

"I was hoping that by the time you discovered it, you'd be so inflamed with passion you wouldn't care."

He found her mouth again, held it for a long, provocative kiss that left Laine breathless. "Kiss me like that again and I probably won't know my name." He laughed softly, and touched his tongue to the seam of her lips. "Murphy," she murmured, tangling her fingers in his hair. "Kiss me like that again."

When it counted most, he could be amazingly obedient. He was also creative. And thorough, the hot urgency of his mouth making her weak with wanting.

His index finger repeatedly drew the neckline of her shirt, at last freeing the top button. He dealt with each button slowly, as if he had all day to finish the task. It was only when he said, "I do have all day. And all night," that Laine realized she'd verbalized the thought.

"You make me say and do crazy things."

"Works both ways."

Though she was still covered by the blouse, he looked down at her hungrily. "I've touched you. Dreamed about you. But I haven't seen you. Yet."

Laine tried to speak and heard her voice, breathless and faint from the promise in his words. "Please. Now."

Murphy drew a ragged breath and slipped the cool fabric down her arms. He brushed it off the bed with one hand. At last, his eyes feasted visually on what he had uncovered. With a raspy whisper, he said, "Watch."

Trembling, fighting the impulse to close her eyes, Laine watched his mouth lightly graze her breast, open, take her in. In her entire life, she had never seen, never felt anything so purely erotic.

His tongue, circling, rubbing over the taut peak, was wildly exciting. But the steady, insistent suction that followed sent live currents flashing through her. She arched into him, offering more of herself, shuddering when his teeth raked gently over the tight, sensitive crest of her nipple.

Murphy caught one of her hands, entwining their fingers, stretching their arms to the side. He shifted to her other breast and his mouth began working the same sweet madness while he stroked and shaped and teased the nipple he had just dampened.

Laine lifted her hips, seeking to ease the sweet ache he'd ignited in her lower body. He thrust once against her thigh before bringing both hands to the waist of her shorts.

Waves of pleasure flowed over Laine, freeing her of inhibitions as easily as he removed her remaining clothing.

His fingertips were like exquisite sensing devices. He knew just how much pressure to exert, just where she was most receptive. "Murphy, I—"

"I know, I know," he assured her softly. "Be patient. It's coming." His fingers danced lightly up her inner thigh, traversed teasingly to the other, repeated the tantalizing play down to her other knee.

"Patience isn't one of my virtues."

"Maybe you should practice it more." He touched her then, where the ache was most intense, trapping the heated dampness with his palm. "Patience, Laine, is its own reward. Didn't you know?" Using the base of his hand, he exerted the slightest force, and his thumb turned bold and dexterous, each circular caress driving her wilder, pushing her higher.

"Stop torturing me, Murphy. Take—" She gave a strangled cry when one finger eased inside and began a gliding motion until she was whimpering, writhing, a mass of unfulfilled desire. She needed him unbearably and his every look, every touch escalated that need. She brushed his aroused flesh and he stiffened.

"Laine? Are you—"

He didn't have to finish the question before she snapped out of the numbing cloud of passion. "Oh, Murphy... we can't. I'm not..." She struggled to explain, dimly aware that there was no delicate euphemism for the subject of birth control. Or lack thereof. She cursed herself for trying to pretend that this wouldn't happen. "Why is it that the time when you least want to think about this is when it's the most important?" She tried to pull away, but his fingers closed around her wrist.

He dropped a soft kiss into her palm. "Sunshine, I've wanted you since the day we met. Doesn't it make sense that I'd be prepared for when the time finally came? I'll take care of you."

Laine wanted to protest, but she was too relieved. She sighed and surrendered herself to Murphy and what had been inevitable since the day they met.

He turned away for a few seconds and then his hands were under her, lifting, guiding. "Take me deep." He was inside her, deep, with one fluid surge of his hips.

His mouth, open over hers, absorbed the breath that he'd forced from her. He didn't move, every muscle tensed. "I wanted you so much. Too much."

"I want you just as desperately. Don't hold back." He made a wild sound that melted any trace of caution left in her.

"No. We'll have all of each other."

He was totally consumed by the act of loving her, and Laine reveled in his absorption. He whispered roughly, urgently, what he wanted to do, then with his hands, his mouth, his gloriously aroused body, proceeded to do every one of them. He kept her poised on the brink of madness, need raging through her like a fire storm.

Murphy had always been able to control his body because his mind retained a measure of detachment. With Laine, he was too involved on every level. Every cell in his body—brain included—clamored for complete release. No longer was his control absolute.

He was whispering wild, explicit intentions, commands, things he'd never said to any woman before. And he was doing them, half-delirious because he wanted this to last forever, shaking because he knew it was almost over.

One word from her swept away what little sanity he still possessed. It came first as a whisper, then a demand.

"Colin. *Colin!*"

"Yes, Yes!" Murphy fought to stall the inevitable when he felt her first contraction pull at him. He stilled, watching, deriving a fierce pleasure from her release. The satisfaction was almost stronger than his own. But as each progressive spasm gripped her and she breathed his name yet again, he was lost. Her release became his, and he gave himself up to the ultimate sharing.

MURPHY KNEW HIS DEAD WEIGHT must be crushing Laine, but he didn't trust his arm to support him. At last he'd recovered enough strength to roll to his side, but he carried her with him, so they were lying face-to-face.

It was a strange sensation—feeling totally depleted and utterly fantastic at the same time. Laine looked almost as dazed as he felt. He gave up trying to contain his smile of satisfaction. "Sunshine, it's a good thing you don't need passion. I don't think I'd have survived otherwise."

Her eyes were still closed. "Don't make fun of me, Murphy," she said around a heavy sigh. "And don't ask me what happened. I don't know."

"You don't?" He nuzzled her neck with extreme gentleness, not wanting her to start having misgivings about the closeness they'd just shared.

"Oh, I know *what* happened. But I don't understand why. I'm not usually so—" Laine looked at him questioningly as she struggled for the right words.

"So abandoned? Uninhibited? How about demanding?"

"All of the above," she admitted with a small moan. "I know you think I'm spontaneous and impulsive, and I guess I am sometimes. But not ever about this." She shivered, goose bumps pebbling her skin.

Murphy levered himself up to find the comforter and tuck it back around them. The room was quite cold now, but he didn't want to risk leaving Laine even for the few seconds it would take to adjust the air conditioner. He wanted to make sure that she didn't regret their lovemaking. And if he was being honest, he needed some reassurance that she'd been as consumed by it as he had.

"If it's any consolation, I was pretty far outside myself, too." He framed her face with both hands and looked deeply into her eyes. "Laine, I want you to know that I don't do this often. In the past few years, I've been pretty reclusive, and that includes from women. But you're different. This meant something. Do you understand? It was—" He stopped and shook his head.

"I know," she said when he seemed unable to come up with the right word. "I'm having trouble finding a superlative for it, too. Maybe I'm in shock."

Relieved, he chuckled and settled onto his back with one hand behind his head. Murphy stared at the ceiling for a few seconds before saying, "Out at the river you told everyone that we had plans. Is this what you had in mind?"

Laine shot him a disbelieving look. "Hardly. After we cleaned up, I meant to let you pick how we spent the rest of the day. It seems that I'm always dragging you along on some misguided escapade and you've been so sweet and cooperative all week. I wanted this afternoon to be your choice."

A laugh rumbled up from his chest as he pulled her onto him. "Guess what we'd have done, Sunshine, if you let me choose whatever I wanted?"

"Gone to the baseball game?" she asked coyly. But her body was quivering from the pleasurable sting of his teeth biting her shoulder.

"Guess again."

His words were muffled against the upper swell of her breast and Laine moaned as his hand lifted and molded her to fit his mouth. "Again?" she gasped as she felt the slick wet sorcery of his tongue and lips sucking her into the vortex of passion. Again.

IT WAS EARLY EVENING when Laine woke. She could tell by the angle and softness of the light coming through the window shades behind her bed. She never took naps during the day. But then, she didn't usually make wild, wanton love three times in a single afternoon either. Her mission the past couple of weeks had been to introduce Murphy to new experiences. Today he'd returned the favor. With interest. She closed her eyes on a smile, and stretched languidly.

"Men usually turn and run when they see smiles like that. They're dangerous."

Her eyes widened when she saw him standing in the doorway. "I don't see you running."

"Maybe I'm a braver man than most."

He crossed to the bed, and it was like replaying a scene from *Indiscreet*. Fingers of one hand wrapped around the neck of a champagne bottle, he clutched the stems of two tulip glasses in the other. Cary Grant had worn a tux and patent leather evening slippers. Murphy was dressed in a clean pair of hip-riding cutoffs and nothing else. But he stretched out on top of the coverlet with the same grace as her movie hero. Laine couldn't remember any man ever looking better to her than Murphy did at that moment.

Her eyes scanned the room, searching for her clothes. She found them, neatly folded, on a corner chair. Too far away. The nudity that had seemed so natural a short time before now made her feel vulnerable.

"Would you like a robe?"

Laine nodded, grateful and a little taken back by Murphy's consideration. He was brash and unselfconscious, so prone to sardonic humor that she'd expected him to taunt her about the sudden modesty. "There's one behind the bathroom door." He found the knee-length peach-colored satin wrap and dropped it in her lap without a word. While she shrugged into it and tied the belt, he busied himself with uncorking the bottle.

He handled it expertly, she noticed, adding up another point in his favor. Murphy could be as suave and accomplished as the best of them, if he wanted. He just didn't bother most of the time. Laine acknowledged that his contrariness fascinated her as much as everything else about him, perhaps more. "I thought you didn't like wine. Or trust people who drink it."

His mouth quirked at her reminder of what he'd said at the cocktail party. He passed her a nearly full glass. "Mmm, but this is champagne. That makes all the difference." He clinked their glasses together. "As you said, champagne is for celebrating."

Reluctant to ask what they were celebrating, Laine took several swallows, letting the cool effervescence trickle down her throat. She leaned back against the fluffy pillows before taking another sample. "Drinking champagne in bed while the sun is still shining seems . . . decadent."

"I know stuff that's even more so." His thumb and index finger grasped her satin lapel and ran the length from collar to sash. With a single deft flick of his wrist, the robe fell open.

Laine's reflex was to cover herself, but his eyes, hot and avid, stopped her. He took a sip from his glass— but didn't swallow—and put his mouth to her breast. Her back arched, then stiffened, and finally she yielded to the sensations washing over her.

"Aaah, God, Murphy! That *is* decadent."

"Just wait. I've been saving up."

MURPHY WOKE, momentarily disoriented. It was barely dawn, and he never woke this early except under duress. The second difference was that his arms were full of soft, pliant woman. Laine. With him. Nothing had ever felt so damned good, so perfectly right. She probably wouldn't see it quite the same way. She wasn't in love with him. Yet. But two weeks ago there couldn't have been a less likely candidate to attract her attention than Colin Murphy. And look where he was now. Diligence, patience always won out.

He let out a contented sigh and pulled her closer. Murphy had discovered mutual sexual satisfaction almost twenty years ago. Until last night he hadn't known squat about fulfillment, shared with the woman he loved. Until, "Laine."

Laine stirred when she heard Murphy whisper her name. But it took her a few seconds to become alert. His eyes were bloodshot, red rimmed and heavy lidded, his lips slack and swollen. He looked as if he'd spent all night doing exactly what he had been. He looked deliciously sexy.

That was the elusive description of him that had flitted around inside her head the day she'd first seen him on the television interview. Not handsome, or even particularly good-looking; not a hunk. Sexy. She might not have been able to put a label on it right away, but her instincts had been on target.

His thumb skimmed along under one of her eyes, which she could feel were as puffy as his. "You didn't get enough sleep."

"Mmm, no," she murmured, snuggling closer to his warmth. Murphy generated enough heat for two. He'd be a wonderful substitute for her electric blanket on cold nights. Laine cautioned herself not to think about such a possibility.

He lightly touched her bottom lip. "You're tender from too many kisses."

"Then one more won't hurt, will it?" She brushed her lips over his.

He resisted her attempts to intensify the kiss. "Your face is red from my beard." The back of his fingers traced the abraded skin along her jaw, down her neck, all the way to her waist and beyond. "Why didn't you stop me?"

A delicate frisson shot through Laine, from where his hand rested low on her stomach to deep inside her. "You were very... involved. I'm not sure the U.S. Marines could have stopped you. Providing I had wanted them to. Which I didn't."

One of his legs insinuated itself between hers. His knee bent, worked upward. "You should try to get some more sleep."

"I will if you will." Laine's hand found his waist, her fingers spread and strayed lower.

"Yes, let's. A couple more hours and we'll—" He inhaled sharply when her hand closed around him, and he answered the caress with one that was equally arousing.

"Murphy, I don't—"

"Yes, you do. And so do I."

His sweet, relentless persuasion convinced Laine that he was right.

7

LATE THAT MORNING, Murphy walked into the sun
room and flopped down on a wildly patterned wicker
love seat. He felt drained of energy, which didn't say
much for his endurance. Obviously getting in shape for
marathons of any kind required a training period. And
a recuperative period. He was glad that Laine didn't
seem any more anxious than he was to rush out and do
something physical. After they'd cooked and eaten
brunch, she'd announced that the most strenuous thing
she planned to do for the rest of the day was read
everything in the Sunday paper. That was almost as
much of a relief as the fact that she hadn't mentioned
anything about him leaving. He propped his feet up on
a brass trunk and leaned his head against the cushion.

Laine smiled when she caught Murphy dozing off.
Poor baby, she thought, feeling very solicitous. He had
worked so hard. Trying not to disturb him, she put the
fat bundle of paper on the trunk beside his feet and began organizing sections in the order in which she liked
to read them.

"What sections do you want?" she asked, when he
opened one eye.

"Just comics and the crossword."

Her hands fumbled with the comics. How could his sleepy-morning voice inundate her with sensual tremors when she was positively sated? Why couldn't she stop her eyes from taking a slow journey? She answered her own rhetorical question. Because everything about his body appealed to her. From his bare feet to his lean, tanned legs that were sprinkled with just the right amount of hair, up to . . . His cutoffs, frayed and faded, graphically emphasized the masculine shape of him. Laine dropped the two sections on his lap.

Her voice wasn't quite steady, but she asked, "Don't you want the main section? Or the business? We've been so busy the past couple of weeks, I've completely lost touch with what's going on."

"I always throw those parts away. If it weren't for the funnies, I wouldn't even take a newspaper." He became instantly absorbed in *Bloom County*.

"But—" This was just another of Murphy's quirks and Laine figured it probably wasn't worth arguing about. "You must get all your news from TV," she guessed, sounding faintly critical.

"Nope. I don't pay attention to any news. It's all bad. Who needs to hear that?"

She didn't really believe that and told herself it didn't matter even if it was true. But she couldn't leave the subject alone. It was a familiar affliction by this time. "You need to keep up with what's going on in the world. Everyone should try to stay informed."

"Why? You can't do a damned thing to change any of it." He yawned and turned a page.

"You probably never vote either," she said accusingly.

"I always vote. For everything, from president to dogcatcher."

"Why bother exercising your constitutional right to vote if you can't change anything?"

"Simple. How else can I complain with a clear conscience?"

There was a flaw somewhere in his argument, but she decided not to belabor a no-win point. "Is that some variation of Murphy's law?"

"You catch on fast, Sunshine. Here," he said, tossing the comics toward her. "Read *Dennis the Menace*. It'll give you a chuckle."

He was right. She did chuckle. Dennis was using Murphy-like logic to make his point with Mr. Wilson. And like Laine, Mr. Wilson finally gave up with a kind of rueful admiration.

She started working her way through the *Journal* when Murphy bent over the puzzle. Laine always saved the crossword for last, a reward for finishing the rest of the paper. But since he was a guest she generously allowed him the privilege. What really irked her was that he did it so fast. Using a pen.

"Show-off," she mouthed. Laine dropped her paper, laughing as she fought the steady barrage of sofa pillows that her remark provoked. When his supply of ammunition was exhausted, she went back to the sports page. Murphy rearranged the pillows, then started to prowl the room, examining her collection of tacky memorabilia. Most of it was courtesy of Claire, but

Laine had acquired several treasures of her own from some of the more exotic places she'd been.

"Aw, now this is too much. You can't be serious," he said, pausing in front of one of the many frames on the only window-free wall in her sun room.

"You don't like Elvis?" It was tricky trying to sound offended when you were biting your tongue to keep from laughing. She didn't have to look up to know what he was objecting to.

"Of course I do. Everyone likes Elvis. But not on black velvet. Laine, this thing is practically obscene."

"How can you say that?" she protested with mock indignation. "The man who sold it to me said it was an original. The only one of its kind."

"Uh, huh. And the minute you drove off, out came another original." He gave the offensive portrait one last glance before moving on to a low bookcase. "Everything in the rest of your house shows class and style. The stuff in this room is a nightmare. How come?"

"Maybe I have a latent sleazy streak." Laine abandoned her attempt at humor when he pinned her with an intolerant glare. "The tackiness lends a sense of balance when I'm in one of my moods. Lonely or sentimental. Sad."

"Most people would think you're always up, always as bright as sunshine."

Laine noticed that Murphy hadn't said *he* thought her incapable of moodiness, just most people. "Don't you believe it. I'm a Gemini. We can change faces just like that." She snapped her fingers. "But you don't have much faith in astrology, I'm sure."

Murphy didn't reply. True, he didn't give much credence to astrology, but he'd always suspected that Laine probably had to work extra hard to be as overwhelmingly cheerful and optimistic as she was. Those kind of people usually had dark spots they were determined to hide. As she was hiding behind the paper right now.

He picked up a heavy album and went back to the love seat. Looking at something this personal could tell him a lot about Laine. He wanted to know everything. Now that they were lovers, Murphy wasn't going to allow their relationship to revert to the easygoing lark it had been before. From this point, he intended for them to work on a future. Together.

Rather than start at the beginning, he opened the book to a random page. Laine in her graduation cap and gown was posed with a handsome couple that he assumed were her parents. The infamous Smokin' Joe and an attractive woman with Laine's coloring. As he turned pages, he saw Laine and Randy Williamson smiling and pointing to the R&R sign on their building. He'd learned last week that Randolph and Randolph was composed of Randy's first and Laine's last names.

Laine and . . . Murphy froze. He felt hot and cold. Sick. Scared. "Who is he, Laine?" he forced himself to ask, dreading the answer.

She came to look over his shoulder, then just as quickly went to the bank of windows that overlooked her backyard. Her spine was rigid, unnaturally so, and she wrapped her arms around herself, as if she were chilled. "His name was Jeff Woodard."

He heard the slight emphasis on *was* and his mind flooded with possible explanations, none of them palatable. He stared at the photograph again. It was just a thirty-five-millimeter snapshot taken of the pair at a party. But it was the way they looked at each other, as if no one else in the world existed, that made Murphy's hands sweat and his stomach turn upside down.

"I don't even need to ask how much you loved each other. I can see it in your eyes. In his." The silence stretched on forever before she spoke.

"Look closely, Murphy. Those aren't my eyes."

He did as she said, and his grip on the album loosened a fraction. At first glance, anyone would have made the same mistake. The differences were minute, but they were there. Especially to Murphy who had spent hours looking at Laine. Why hadn't she mentioned something this important? "You have a twin sister."

"Had. Maureen. She's dead. And so is Jeff."

She sounded so tough and brittle, not at all like the Laine he knew. The stark words were too calculated, as if she'd recited them from a prepared script. One she had practiced a lot.

Murphy went to stand close to her, but didn't touch. "I imagine it's very hard to talk about it." Some previously undetected sixth sense told him that she needed to talk about it. The intuition also told him that her sister's death somehow represented a barrier between him and the future he wanted with Laine.

She whirled around to confront him, her gaze coolly detached. "There's nothing to talk about. She's dead and I've dealt with it."

He looked at her for a long time, and Laine could feel herself weakening, yearning to say more. But she couldn't, had never been able to discuss Maureen with anyone. Not even Claire, the person closest to her, knew that after two years she still harbored feelings of helplessness and guilt about her sister's death.

"All right," he said quietly, as if he recognized and accepted her inability to share it with him. "Not yet."

Left unsaid was the admonition, "Soon."

Keenly aware that Murphy was allowing her to evade the issue of her sister, Laine tried desperately to restore the light, playful tone that had dissolved so quickly when he'd discovered the photograph. "Want to walk over to the club and go swimming?" she asked with forced enthusiasm.

In a voice that was utterly calm and so quiet she could barely hear, he said, "It won't work, you know."

Laine sank back into her chair, exhausted, but strangely keyed up. "What won't work? Swimming?"

"No, the diversion. I don't want to go swimming and neither do you." One quelling shake of his head silenced her objection before she could voice it. "I respect your right not to discuss Maureen, but that doesn't mean I'll let you lapse back into the butterfly act. You've been dancing just out of reach since we got up."

She wanted to tell him she didn't know what he was talking about, but such an outright lie was impossible.

While the precise nature and extent of her feelings for Murphy had yet to be defined, she'd already made love with him. Repeatedly and voraciously. Never having experienced anything similar, Laine was unprepared to handle a relationship like hers and Murphy's. It had begun against all odds and blazed into her life like a comet. She'd always believed that love evolved out of mutual interests and time spent together. The physical part would come as a natural extension of those other, deeper emotions. *Love!* she thought, shaken. She really was in deep water if it had come to that. Love was a factor Laine couldn't deal with right now.

Curbing her panicky reaction, she asked, "What do you want to do?" A memory from the day before flooded her, made her regret her choice of words. *Guess what we'd have done, Sunshine, if you let me choose whatever I wanted?*

"I want to talk about why you're trying to ignore that we spent yesterday afternoon, last night and part of this morning making such soul-shattering love that I thought I was dying. Over and over. I've never felt like that, Laine."

"Murphy, please."

He sat forward, silencing her with his golden gaze. "Colin. You called me that for the first time ever, just before you—" He stopped when he heard her shocked intake of breath. "I don't know why, but that sent me over the edge." He leaned across the brass trunk between them and clasped one of her hands. "I know you're not ready to talk about the feelings that made it inevitable. I can live with that for now. But I'm damned sure not going to let you treat it like a tea party. We shared a bed, Sunshine, and everything that's implied."

Why did she keep forgetting that his indolence was deceptive? He could pounce with the swiftness of a panther. And he didn't pull any punches. She matched him with reckless bravado. "Believe me, I'm well aware that we shared a bed. Every time I move, secret places I didn't even know I had remind me."

The hand that held hers tensed. "I hurt you? God, Laine, I'm sorry. Did you tell me? Didn't I listen?"

He released her hand and threaded his fingers together. She could see one foot pumping up and down, a sign Laine now recognized as nervous agitation. His concern was touching, but misplaced. "You didn't hurt me, Murphy." She touched his knee and gave him a reassuring smile. "I think it's a simple case of overworking muscles that have been dormant for a long time." A very long time in her case.

"You're sure?" Only when she nodded and whispered, "Sure," did he relax. At last the ghost of a smile met hers. "I've got a few of those muscles myself. In case you haven't noticed, I'm not moving up to speed today."

"Then what do you say to a snail-paced walk around the neighborhood? It'll do us both good."

They went into the bedroom to collect shoes and the key ring from her tote. Laine made it a point not to look at the bed, which was now neatly made, camouflaging what had taken place earlier. But it was on her mind and, she was positive, on Murphy's. Only moments ago, he'd been determined to make her face the reality of what they'd done. She locked the door, certain that her reprieve was temporary.

A predawn shower had dissipated yesterday's mugginess and lowered the temperature slightly. The small front yards were green and glistening. Petunias and geraniums stood fresh and colorful, rescued from the torpor of unseasonable heat.

Murphy looked closely at Laine's neighborhood, seeing it in a different light because she was a part of it. "You know, I've never shared this rabid fascination with Ansley Park. It's interesting architecturally, and I like the wide streets and flowers planted in the circles. But the houses are too close together, the yards too small." He toyed with the idea of whether he could bear to live in such confining surroundings. Maybe about half the time. If he could be with Laine.

"I guess you've got a point," she said, sounding a shade defensive. "It seems like the perfect family neighborhood to me. But then I don't have much to compare it with."

"You moved around a lot, I guess," he speculated, aware that he'd blundered onto a sensitive subject. He draped his arm around her shoulders and gave her a little squeeze, trying to tell her that he understood.

"We lived in so many places that I doubt I could name them all. Selective memory, probably. The four years I spent at Tech were the longest I'd ever been in one place. I got used to stability. And Atlanta. Now it's home."

Murphy knew how important home was to him. He imagined it would be even more so for Laine given her family's nomadic life-style.

After walking a couple of irregularly shaped blocks, they came to tiny McLatchey Park. Laine waved to a pair of teenage boys during a point break in their tennis game. Then she and Murphy made their way to the small playground and claimed two swings.

"I drew up the plans for some friends who did a gut rehab over on The Prado," he said casually. He had even attended the open house they'd given to celebrate the renovation. It was eerie to realize he'd been so close to Laine less than a year ago. "Did you have to do a lot of work on your house?"

"Nothing major, fortunately. I refinished the wood floors, painted everything and had my first taste of wallpapering. It was fun, but I wouldn't want to make a career of it."

Murphy chuckled. He liked coming up with the ideas, but he wasn't crazy about doing detailed finish work, either. He was hoping Laine would be curious enough to ask where he lived. Now was the perfect time to lay a little groundwork. But it looked as if he'd have to wait a while for that.

He could handle that. Time and patience would overcome Laine's reservations. He had enough of both. The timetable was the only element in question because he knew what the final outcome would be.

Murphy got up and stood behind her. "Hold on," he said, and began pushing. He didn't push hard or high, just a series of gentle shoves that kept the swing returning to his hands every few seconds.

Laine quickly got caught up in the action and began pumping her legs to gain more height on each arc. Within a few passes she was soaring, giddy with excitement at the simple pleasure. "Higher, Murphy! Faster!"

He obliged until, dizzy, she laughed and shouted, "Stop. I can't take any more."

He slowed her gradually until she was barely moving. Then, with his hands resting on her shoulders, his mouth close to her ear, he said, "Now tell me, why the ostrich act? We're more than buddies, Laine. We're lovers, and I'd like you to at least acknowledge that fact."

Laine let go of the chains and studied her hands. Unable to see his face, his eyes, she couldn't gauge his mood. Regardless of whether he was angry or merely puzzled, he had a right to question her ostrich act, as he'd termed it. She just wasn't sure she had the answer.

"Actually, ever since I woke, I've been trying to tell myself that I should say something like, 'Murphy, that shouldn't have happened, can't happen again. We just got carried away, caught up in the mood of the movie.'"

"I suppose you could build a case using that as a motivation."

Laine sat very still, waiting.

"How many times have you seen *Indiscreet*?"

He sounded only remotely curious, but she could already guess where he was headed. "I've probably watched it at least twenty times."

He walked around in front of her and pulled her to her feet. "Ever made love as soon as the movie ended, because it put you in the mood?"

"Uh, no." Neither had she ever watched it with a nude male in her bed.

His eyes were gleaming, alive with anticipation. "Ever been tempted?"

"No," she replied honestly. As much as she enjoyed the story of Ingrid Bergman's and Cary Grant's romance, it had never before held any aphrodisiac powers for her. It had taken Murphy to provide that.

"Then I think we have to conclude that we're together because of a pretty meaningful attraction to each other."

Laine said nothing, unable to deny his statement, yet reluctant to admit just how true it was. Her hands shook; she had an abnormal urge to cry.

"Sunshine, this thing between us isn't about sex. I know it, and I think you do, too. I want more than that from you. I need more."

She leaped up from the swing and headed toward home, wishing she could turn the clock back twenty-four hours. "Don't crowd me. I can't handle it right now."

He was right behind her. "I'm trying not to push. But I can't let you run from me. We need to spend time together, learn more about each other."

She'd been afraid of this. "I know you're going to badger me to spill all the gory details about Maureen, but I simply don't discuss that. Not with anyone." The note of incipient hysteria in her voice was alarming.

"I don't want you to *spill* anything, Laine. I want you to share with me, whatever and whenever it feels right. Because I care about you," he said with quiet certainty. "And whether you admit it or not, you care about me, too. At least a little bit."

She kept her head down, tracking each step. "I tried so hard, Murphy," she said plaintively. "All last week, and when we were in the mountains, I tried to keep my distance."

He stopped and made her face him. She looked up into his eyes, eyes that could make her forget every good intention.

"I know you did. But don't you see, it didn't make any difference. That's why we're here. Why I'm not leaving."

Another variation of Murphy's law, Laine supposed. So far, she'd been totally inept at deflecting him when he wanted something. But she had to try. "Surely you have business that needs your attention. You've been away two weeks. I'll be glad to take you to the airport."

A phantom smile vanished as quickly as it appeared. "I have all the time this is going to take, Sunshine. You're much too eager to get rid of me. Haven't you learned it's not that easy?"

If she didn't already know it, Laine was catching on quickly. She again struck out at a lively pace. The protection of her home was within sight now. Except that Murphy had invaded that, too.

"You can take me by the hotel so I can check out and pick up the rest of my luggage."

Was he suggesting that one night entitled him to move in with her? He hadn't exactly said so, but Laine got the impression that was his plan. "I offered you a ride to the airport. Since you're not interested in that, I'll drive you to Colony Square. You're on your own from there." She heard how haughty and abrupt her dismissing words sounded, but couldn't stop herself. Jamming the key into the lock, she said, "In fact, just let me grab my purse and we'll go now." She picked up a small red shoulder bag from a table beside the front door and led him to the Corvette.

As if by design, he'd picked the hotel closest to Ansley Park. As a result, the drive was far too short for Laine to resolve the dilemma of what she was going to do with Murphy. Her teeth chewed on her bottom lip as she made the final turn. Still preoccupied, she had to jam on the brakes and screech to a halt.

"I don't know what happens next either, Laine," Murphy said softly. "But whatever it is, we'll decide together. I just can't face staying in this damned hotel another night. If you don't want me at your place, I can make other arrangements. After we talk about the alternatives. Wait for me. I won't be gone long."

He opened the door and put one foot out before changing his mind. "But first." His hand curved around her neck, drawing her to him. With an expertise perfected by familiarity, his mouth took hers. Lips caressing, tongue stroking, Murphy rekindled the explosive desire that burned hot, and seemingly unquenchable, between them. Laine forgot where they were, instantly lost in the wonder only he could create.

By the time he pulled away, she was dazed, trembling, wanting more. His gaze took in the lambent glow in her eyes, her lips parted and moistened by his own. "There," he said, satisfied with his handiwork. "Maybe—just maybe—that will hold me until I get back. If I hurry." With that he was gone, a springy step negating his earlier reference to being slow today. At that moment, it would have taken a bomb threat to transplant Laine. Only her eyes moved, charting his course to the hotel door.

At the sight of his languidly graceful movements, a wave of yearning crashed through her. Murphy's powerful sensuality was cleverly masked by his querulous outward demeanor and a flagrant disregard for fashion. But Laine was so attuned to him now that she wondered why it had taken her several days to pick up on his subtle erotic messages. They'd been there all along—in the stance of his body, openly inviting, or with a look that said, "I want you and I can make you want me." Even in his veiled warning on that first night in the mountains. "What I want, I take."

He had taken Laine, and she him, over and over, pushing their minds and bodies to the outer limits of reason, and beyond. Nothing in her life had prepared Laine for the intensity of what she and Murphy had shared. And she knew with absolute certainty that nothing, nobody, would ever again affect her as profoundly as Colin Murphy.

The uniformed bellhop gave Murphy a snappy salute as he opened the door for him. From the grin on his young face and the inclination of his head toward her car, Laine guessed he'd passed along some man-to-man comment. Averting her eyes, she caught a glimpse of herself in the rearview mirror.

It was a look she had seen before.

Her fingers clutched desperately at the steering wheel; her breathing accelerated audibly. "No," she whispered shakily, then the plea grew louder. "Oh, no!" Laine could not force herself to meet the reflection again, terrified of what she would see. One fleeting impression was enough to haunt her for a lifetime.

The woman in the mirror had been gazing at Murphy with the same adoration in her eyes that Laine's sister had focused on her fiancé. The same all-consuming adoration that had foretold Maureen's downfall.

And now it was happening to Laine, too.

In spite of the late afternoon sun's heat, a bone-chilling dampness spread over her. But Laine's hands were paralyzed, unable to massage any warmth into her leaden arms. A foggy corner of her brain tried to insist that this couldn't be real. She had vowed never to fall into the same self-destructive pattern that had claimed her sister. Laine would not allow herself to become so involved with or obsessed by any man that she couldn't face a life without him.

Maureen had been brilliant, graduating at the top of her medical-school class, but she was also driven. She had to excel, to be the best at whatever she undertook. Perhaps it was a compensation for being shy and insecure in social situations and personal relationships.

Laine recalled how shocked she'd been at her sister's transformation after Maureen had met Jeff Woodard.

In love for the first time, Maureen had bloomed, openly confiding to Laine the depth of passion she'd found with Jeff, how he'd made her a real woman at last. "Eternally, wonderfully terrifying," had been her words.

Everyone had liked Jeff. He was a fun-loving optimist, kind and decent, generous to a fault, loving and devoted to Maureen. He had acted as her anchor, her ground to reality. Until the night he'd been shot at point-blank range by some deranged maniac he had stopped to help on a freeway.

Unable to recover from her combined grief and guilt, Maureen had chosen not to go on living without the man she loved so obsessively. It was all such a waste.

No woman should be so dependent on a man that she couldn't endure life without him. It was unhealthy, dangerous. Potentially fatal. Helpless, Laine had witnessed love's ravaging power. And yet, she'd been looking at Murphy through the same eyes with which Maureen had viewed Jeff.

Laine's heart seemed swollen to twice its size, filling her chest, choking her while it made breathing impossible. Her hands shook uncontrollably and she feared she might black out any second.

Murphy, her growing attachment to him, had brought her here. If she could get away from him, she could save herself from the same fate that had driven Maureen to suicide. She had to run. It was her only hope of salvation. Laine groped blindly for the ignition key, reciting a silent prayer.

MURPHY HAD CALLED AHEAD to the hotel earlier in the day. His bill required only a signature and his luggage was waiting at the registration desk. The whole procedure took less than five minutes. When he exited with his leather garment bag slung over his shoulder, he felt ready to deal with any obstacle Laine threw in his path.

Except flight.

He heard the ominous rumble of her Stingray, followed by screaming tires as she sent the car streaking down the hotel's drive.

Illogically, his first thought was that she'd been right. Four-hundred-and-twenty-seven cubic inches of displacement could lay an impressive strip of rubber.

Then the anger hit.

8

MURPHY'S JAW MUSCLES tightened in silent fury. What the hell kind of number was she trying to do on him? Did she think he'd let her get by with leaving him in a cloud of dust? Not bloody likely. He had warned her that getting rid of him wasn't going to be simple.

Murphy impatiently hailed the first cab in the lineup. "You gotta fifty-buck tip if you don't lose that 'Vette'," he said, tossing his bag into the backseat and jumping in right behind. "Move it, pal!"

"Aw' right!" the cabbie agreed gleefully, his Checker Marathon hurtling forward in a poor imitation of Laine's Corvette. "Any idea where she's headed?"

"Could be Ansley Park. But don't count on it. I think the lady's spooked."

"No sweat, man. I know this town. She's as good as yours with Jarvis at the wheel." Jarvis blew a big pink bubble as he shot through a yellow-turning-red light on Peachtree at the High Museum and switched lanes to squeeze in behind Laine's car. "Don't worry. We'll stick to her like white on rice."

His initial flush of anger disintegrating, Murphy settled back to contemplate what had made Laine bolt. Something had shaken her badly enough that she'd abandoned him without a word of justification. She might be impetuous, but he didn't believe she habitually left people stranded.

Dimly aware that Jarvis displayed an excessive fondness for the cab's horn, Murphy considered possibilities. The one that kept recurring brought a satisfied smile to his face. Early on, Laine had tried to assign him the role of manageable buddy. Only her ploy had backfired. Nobody who knew Murphy would mistake him for manageable. He'd gotten too close last night, and this morning had stumbled onto that picture of her sister. Whatever had happened to Maureen, Laine was determined to guard her feelings about it. While Murphy was willing to give her time to reveal that secret, he had pressured her about continuing their relationship. She had probably weighed all those factors while she waited for him. And then ran for cover.

With the Stingray blazing a trail, they bypassed all the entrances to Laine's neighborhood and continued up Peachtree. At Brookwood Station the cab left squealing tires and fist-shaking drivers in its wake. Murphy had to give old Jarvis credit. He was true to his word. If they got any closer, Laine would never ditch them because their bumpers would be locked. Which probably wouldn't help his case much. "I think it's safe to ease off a little bit."

"Your choice, man," Jarvis said, shrugging as he dropped back about a foot. "She your old lady or something?"

Murphy chuckled at the description. "Let's just say I'm working on it." He returned to his analysis of the situation. He figured he didn't stand a chance until

Laine saw him as a genuine threat to her safe, sanitized prescription for a husband. Only when she started to question his place in her life could she begin to realign her priorities. If she had panicked and run, it meant she now recognized his power to upset her well-ordered plans. Encouraged by this development, he rubbed his hands together and plotted his course.

Murphy had realized this morning that his court-ship of Laine wasn't going to progress to an immediate and effortless culmination. But it was going to end up the way he wanted, no matter what he had to endure. At the moment, surviving Jarvis's driving appeared to be his biggest challenge. Horn blaring, they barreled through another intersection. The light was indisputably red.

"Ah hah!" the cabbie announced, as though he'd solved a complicated mystery. "She's turning into Peachtree Battle. What you wanna do now?"

Without waiting for orders he whipped into the shopping center, too. Murphy's head slammed against the cab's top when Jarvis raced down the steep entrance.

"Hang back until she parks," he said, massaging his head with one hand while digging for his wallet with the other. "Let's see where she goes." When Laine got out and locked her door, Murphy slapped some money into Jarvis's hand and shouldered his leather bag. "Thanks, *man*."

The cabbie grinned, obviously appreciating his passenger's ironic inflection. "Thanks, yourself. Hey," he called, cranking down the window. "You sure you don't want me to wait? I'm beating it back to the hotel. This time I won't even put the meter on."

Murphy only paused a few seconds to shake his head. "I'll be leaving with . . . my old lady." Come hell or high water, Laine wasn't going to escape a second time.

LAINE WAS HALFWAY TO BUCKHEAD before she got control of herself and realized that she was speeding recklessly along one of Atlanta's busiest streets. To make matters worse, for the past several blocks a demented taxi driver had tried his best to crawl up her exhaust pipe. He must be hauling a type-A fare, but no one had to get anywhere in that much of a hurry. Detouring into the shopping center served dual purposes. It got her out of that lunatic's path and helped her to turn around, which she had to do anyway. In her haste to escape, she'd given no thought to a destination.

As long as she was here, she might as well pick up some things at the drugstore. She needed to occupy her mind with a mundane chore. Although she'd calmed down enough to be functional, she wasn't ready to face all the repercussions of the past twenty-four hours. Especially what she'd just done to Murphy.

Laine claimed a shopping cart and began working her way through the maze. Tweezers. Cotton balls. Bloodred nail polish. She'd have to contact Murphy, of course. It was inexcusable to desert him so brusquely. She owed him the courtesy of an explanation. *Brilliant deduction, Laine, but exactly what are you going to say?* Birdseed. Powder puffs. Moist heating pad.

You simply repeat what you said this morning. Going to bed was a mistake that can't happen again. Soap. Chlorine bleach. Collapsible clothesline. *There's only one way to make sure that it won't.* Pens. Rubber bands. Two paperback novels.

That was only the beginning. She could go on all night, enumerating reasons why they had to stop seeing each other. Laine paused. There must be something else she ought to add. "Oh, brother!" she muttered, eyes focused straight ahead. She was standing in front of the display of contraceptives. The one thing she *didn't* need. She shoved her squeaky-wheeled, crab-stepping cart to the next aisle. Razor. After-shave. Athletic supporter.

We both know that I want to get married. Since you're not a candidate, whatever attraction we feel has to end now. Clock. TV Guide. Six rolls of film.

Laine started unloading her booty at the checkout. We're only human, Murphy. Things got a little out of control, but we're adults. Jawbreakers? *One night in bed doesn't mean anything.*

"That'll be eighty-seven ninety-four," the clerk droned nasally.

"I beg your pardon?" Laine said, surveying her mound of purchases while she unzipped her purse. "There must be some mistake." The clerk repeated the exorbitant total, and for the first time Laine ran a mental tab on the pile before her.

There was no mistake in the amount. And no mistaking that she'd picked up the wrong handbag. The one she'd brought had no wallet, no checkbook, no plastic. Damned Murphy!

"Good thing I followed you, huh, Sunshine?"

Laine jumped at the soft, gravelly voice and gaped at the hundred-dollar bill that materialized in her hand. She was literally speechless. Murphy here? How? Why wasn't he yelling at her instead of sounding amused, almost cheerful? He acted as if this unscheduled shopping trip was some kind of game. And he was loaning her a lot of money to pay for a pile of essentially useless items. Tooth-destroying candy and an athletic supporter, of all things. What had possessed her to gather such an assortment of junk? She'd have to return it another time. Right now she was too flustered to think coherently.

After handing Murphy his change, Laine experimented with various word combinations to phrase her apology. It was going to be sticky justifying her actions without telling him the whole truth. But that was out of the question. She could only do her best and hope he'd accept it. Maybe she'd try temporary insanity.

Once they were out of the drugstore, she again wrestled with her conscience about what to do about Murphy. Somehow she had to atone for slipping away from the hotel like a sneak thief. Which meant she couldn't leave him stranded in a shopping center parking lot. Likewise she couldn't just haul him back to Colony Square and dump him on the curb. Resigned to her fate, Laine led Murphy to the car and watched him stow his bag and her ill-gotten purchases in the hatchback. A short while later, they were back at her house. She had rationalized that she wasn't in any state to discuss her recent behavior and concentrate on driving at the same time.

Her apprehension was unfounded. Not only did Murphy not demand an explanation, he wouldn't even allow her to begin one. He dismissed her crazy, irresponsible act as if it had never happened. That baffled Laine and left her wondering where their extraordinary entanglement would lead next.

"I know why you panicked earlier and felt you had to get away," Murphy was saying calmly. "And I understand." They were sitting in her living room, facing each other from two pale lemon-colored love seats that flanked the fireplace. The way Murphy was taking charge of their conversation, Laine felt as if she were the guest. "We haven't known each other very long and you're probably right. We got carried away."

Laine couldn't believe her ears. In a million years she'd never have expected him to say that. To, in effect, agree with her own poor excuse.

"We had a good thing going, just being friends," he went on. "I really enjoyed our time together the past couple of weeks. It doesn't make sense to let anything heavy interfere with our friendship."

She cleared her throat, a prelude to saying something, though what, she wasn't sure. She could try, "You're right, Murphy, sex and friendship don't mix." Except that for them, it had mixed very well. Too well. "What are you suggesting?" she finally got out in a rusty voice.

He propped one ankle on his opposite knee. His incessant picking at the fringe of his cutoffs was the only sign that Murphy was less than completely relaxed. "The solution is simple. We'll go back to the way things were before, uh, before yesterday."

"You think that's possible?" He had offered her the way out of an awkward situation. Why hadn't she agreed and left it at that?

"We're adults," he reasoned. "You said it yourself, passion isn't on your shopping list, even for a husband. And, God knows, I'm capable of being celibate for long periods. I think we can keep our hands off each other."

If this whole scene wasn't so bizarre, Laine would have laughed at its absurdity. Twenty-four hours ago they'd both been so caught up in passion they couldn't have kept their hands to themselves under penalty of death. Today he was deeming passion unnecessary. Murphy's offhand dismissal of the lovemaking she'd found so exceptional annoyed, then angered Laine. But after brief consideration, her insides warmed.

Whatever his motives, he was lying. His nervousness and the fact that he wouldn't look at her was all the proof she needed.

"Sunshine, you're the best friend I've got right now. I don't want to lose you."

He said it with such little-boy sincerity that Laine melted. His earnestness was probably contrived, but she was such a patsy for Murphy that it didn't matter. He was offering her a nonthreatening way to spend a little more time with him, and she was rash enough to grab it. Every time she'd faced saying goodbye, Laine had felt empty. Just a while longer, she bargained. "My lack of willpower around you is disgraceful," she complained.

He sent her a too-innocent smile. "You're on vacation this week, aren't you?"

She nodded, sensing a proposition. "I have the next two weeks off."

"What do you say to doing me a favor?"

He didn't waste time imposing on their resurrected friendship. "That depends on the favor, of course."

Murphy leaned forward, as if they were plotting a conspiracy. "Next Saturday is my brother's wedding, and I have to go up to Hilton Head and play best man."

Laine grinned at her mental image of him standing at the altar in his patented Hawaiian-print shirt. "What does that have to do with me?"

"I was thinking maybe you could come too, and run interference for me with the clan."

"You don't get along with your family?" Acting as referee in a domestic squabble was not Laine's idea of vacation fun.

"Aw, we get along okay. But this wedding promises to be a bigger dose of them than I can tolerate." He eyed her solemnly. "Every time I'm around them, they start in one me about my . . . shortcomings. If I bring you, they'll assume we're . . . well, involved. Mistakenly of course," he added, pointing his index finger for emphasis. "But it'll be enough to keep them off my back."

"What shortcomings are you guilty of?" Laine wondered if Murphy's family could be as exacting as her father, The General.

"Being almost thirty-seven and single is my first offense. Having combined that with the facts that I never show up at family functions with a date in tow and live in blissful solitude, they're convinced I hate women."

"Are they right?"

"Of course not. I don't hate women in general. But I usually have trouble with them in the specific. I'm not very charming by nature. Or handsome, good-humored and tolerant—all those traits that females favor." He shrugged. "Course, I'm equally abrasive to men. I guess there's no help for me."

"Murphy, you don't do self-effacing very well," Laine said, laughing. "You'd best try a different tack."

"But you will come with me?"

"All right," she agreed, weakening. "I was planning to visit Claire, but I can put it off until the following week."

As easily as Murphy had convinced Laine to postpone her own plans and accompany him to South Carolina, he talked her into letting him spend Sunday night at her house. It sounded so practical when he brought up the advantage of getting an early start. He'd sleep upstairs, as he should have the previous night. She didn't have a thing to worry about. They were friends, remember? Laine could trust him.

True enough, for the remainder of the evening there were no hot looks, no erotic signals, no hint that they were anything other than buddies. At bedtime, he climbed the stairs without a word of complaint and stayed there until she was dressed and in the kitchen the next morning. Nothing in his manner gave Laine cause to toss restlessly into the wee hours, reliving every moment of their time together in the bed, which suddenly seemed too large for her alone.

Murphy evidently wasn't bothered by the same tormenting visions. He looked so disgustingly fresh that she asked if he minded driving. That was a measure of how muzzy-headed she was. Laine never trusted anyone at the wheel of her Corvette.

By the time they stopped at Mrs. Wilkes's Boarding House in Savannah for lunch, she was feeling more herself. Enough so that when several people spoke to Murphy, she asked how they knew him. He merely stared at his plate and said, "I do get around some, you know."

Laine chewed on that, along with a fluffy biscuit dripping in butter and peach preserves. Something about his apparent familiarity with Savannah struck her as out of place. But before she could quiz him, Murphy ladled some more food onto her plate from the homestyle serving bowls, and told her to eat up so they could get back on the road.

The drive after lunch took less than two hours and Laine found herself looking forward to meeting Murphy's family. A whole clan, as he'd called them, of cranky skeptics like him promised to be an interesting experience.

A bridge took them over the Intercoastal Waterway to Hilton Head Island, and Murphy directed Laine toward Sea Pines Plantation on the Atlantic side. A couple of turns led them along a lagoon, and finally he pointed to a pair of pineapple gate finials flanking a driveway.

"Oh, Murphy, this is lovely. Did you design it?"

"Nope. I wasn't very old when we moved here. A neighbor just up the way designed it from my mother's ideas. She's from New Orleans and this style reflects that." Laine pulled into the entrance court, absorbing the beauty of Murphy's childhood home. All the years her family had spent moving in and out of quarters—some luxurious, some barely habitable—she'd dreamed of a home such as this.

Nestled among a thick stand of tall pines and palms, it was two stories with a high-pitched roof and wide verandas around the second-floor gallery. The front courtyard was surrounded by crepe myrtle and azaleas; jasmine twined around brick columns that supported the upper veranda.

Murphy pulled out his key ring and unlocked the door to a herringbone-patterned brick entry hall that stretched the entire depth of the house. Immediately they heard a clamor of voices in the distance. He groaned. "I guess the fireworks have already started. If it gets too noisy for you, just make a break for the water. I'll probably be right behind you." He led her past a freestanding spiral staircase to French doors. "Unfortunately, it sounds like they've beaten us to it." The volume increased with each step. "We may as well go find out what the crisis is."

Trees arched together high overhead to shade a brick path that led to the ocean. At the seaward end, a copper eagle weather vane stood watch where the walkway connected with a deck snuggled into the dunes. That's where they were gathered. Murphy hadn't exaggerated: it was a clan. And all of them seemed to be talking at once, punctuating their opinions with hand gestures.

"Oh, Colin," exclaimed a woman that Laine assumed was his mother. She detached herself from the group and came to meet them. "Thank heaven you're here at last. Now maybe we can get something done."

"Hello, Mom. It's nice to see you, too," he replied in a sardonic greeting.

She appeared momentarily abashed, then gave Murphy a contrite smile and stood on tiptoe to kiss his cheek. "Hello, darling. Sorry. I'm so pixilated today."

Laine had never heard anyone use that word as a self-description. The woman looked young to have a thirty-six-year-old child. Rich brown hair, barely touched by silver, and her low, husky drawl were the only family traits Laine could detect that mother and son shared.

"Oh, dear," she said, seeming to notice Laine's presence for the first time. "You've brought someone. A woman. How . . . surprising. How delightful!"

Laine traded amused glances with Murphy after introductions were performed, while Sybil Murphy was still patting her hand. "Come meet the rest," she urged. Laine started forward, but couldn't help overhearing his mother whisper a reprimand, "Colin, try not to act so

inappropriately with this one. She has real potential."
Laine didn't know whether to laugh or run.

Murphy's siblings stopped arguing long enough to
be properly introduced. His sister Susan claimed the
five-and-seven-year-old "hoydens" cavorting noisily in
the surf a few yards away. Josh pointed with pride to the
baby who snoozed in a carrier, dreamily oblivious to
the din around him. Stephen was the epitome of a har-
ried prospective groom; Caroline, his fiancée, was obviously distraught. Erica, the family's twenty-five-year-
old baby, sported a new engagement ring.

The two daughters favored Sybil, but Josh and Stephen studied Laine with the same spectacular eyes that
she found so irresistible in Murphy.

"I presume all this uproar concerns the wedding,"
Murphy said to Erica. "If I were you, Squirt, I'd consider eloping."

She looked from him to Laine, then back, her smile
slyly reminiscent of Murphy's. "Are *you* considering
eloping, Big Brother?"

Laine had never seen Murphy embarrassed—had
supposed it was impossible. But a flush bled through
his tan, coloring his face and neck. His mother inter-
vened at that moment, sparing him a reply.

"Colin, your father's in Japan until the day before the
wedding. You've got to do something. Caroline is beside herself. The florist says he can't possibly get the
special orchids he promised months ago."

Murphy's father was apparently much like Laine's,
rarely around to deal with family crises. But unlike

Laine's mother, Sybil relied on her son to find a solution.

"I don't suppose Caroline has considered using some other flower as an alternative," Murphy suggested mildly.

"Men," Sybil said, looking to Laine for support. "They simply don't understand how important her wedding day is to a bride. Everything must be perfect. We women know."

Laine didn't know, so she smiled noncommittally. Privately she thought Murphy's recommendation sounded sensible. But she didn't understand why they thought it was his responsibility to solve the problem in the first place. Regardless, he got all the details from Caroline, then disappeared inside the house for the better part of an hour.

When he returned, all the arrangements had been made. The orchids would arrive at Charleston airport two days before the ceremony. His only comment was, "I trust one of you can be there to pick them up." With that, he kicked off his shoes, motioned for Laine to follow suit and spirited her away for a hike up the beach.

She was itching to ask him about the strange scenario she'd just witnessed, but kept her curiosity to herself. For one thing, Murphy didn't seem inclined to discuss it. Since she didn't want him probing into her family's peculiarities, she gave him the same courtesy.

"It must have been wonderful growing up here," Laine said, bending to dig out a small shell partially buried in the sand. "The volatile ocean at your back door, a mirrorlike lagoon out the front, and in between, plenty of woods for hiding out."

He gave her an incisive look, then smiled. "That's almost exactly how I'd describe it. It spoiled me, I guess. I hated leaving, especially to go somewhere crowded and noisy and cold." Overhead a flock of gulls flitted noisily. Murphy raised his hand high and one dared to swoop down toward it, veering away only at the last second when it saw there was no food.

"I'm surprised you didn't come back here to live."

He laughed, turning his face up to the sun. "Too much family interference. Besides I've got something better. Maybe you can see it sometime."

"Perhaps," she said cautiously. Laine couldn't imagine anywhere being better, but she would like to see the spot he was referring to.

"There must have been some benefits to a childhood like yours," Murphy prodded. "Surely you've lived in a few interesting places."

"Oh, sure," Laine acknowledged. "I went to summer camp in Switzerland and skied the Alps on Christmas vacations. My French baby-sitter gave me music lessons and our German neighbor taught me how to drive his Porsche."

"Ah, the source of your speed fixation comes to light at last."

"Mmm. But all that isn't an equal trade-off, Murphy." Laine stopped and stared out to sea, tucking her fingers into the back pockets of her peppermint green denim slacks. "I want *my* children to have one place that they can always call home."

"Yes, I agree that's best." His hand curved around her neck and kneaded, his touch gentle and without sensuality. It was comforting and reassuring, and Laine had to remind herself not to get used to it.

They walked at least a mile farther, then turned around. Before they got back to the deck, however, Murphy diverted her into the woods. "I want to show you something."

His something was a tree-house, cleverly placed so as to be nearly invisible to a passerby. Hidden in the canopy of several live oaks and accessible only via a well-concealed ladder, it was the perfect hideaway.

"My first design," Murphy announced. He scaled the ladder, quick and agile, then smiled down an invitation. "Check it out?"

Laine followed. They sat facing each other, cross-legged on the smooth platform floor. He had installed windows to form the upper half of three sides; a solid panel slid along a track to enclose the fourth.

"For years, this has been my special place. Where I escape to when I can't take the noise anymore. It's off limits to everyone else in the family."

Laine guessed very few people had ever been invited to share Murphy's private space, here or anywhere else. "I guess you always wanted to be an architect," she speculated, leaning against one wall.

"Not a chance. When I was in fifth grade, my teacher said I was a born architect because I was mathematically and visually inclined. But when she told me it would take another twelve years of education, I nixed the whole idea. I hated school."

She sat up, interested. In spite of his tendency to deny it, Murphy was one of the most intelligent men Laine had ever met. "Something obviously changed your mind."

"In high school, my parents made me take a battery of aptitude tests. After five days, the verdict was that I was a born architect." He ducked his head, but she saw mischief in his eyes. "Naturally I said, 'No way will I *ever* go into architecture.'"

"Because you're that perverse?"

"Because I wanted to write songs," he said simply.

Oddly enough, she could imagine him succeeding at that, too. "I give up. What gave you that final push?"

Murphy grinned sheepishly. "There was this girl in high school. I'd been admiring her from afar. One day she confided that she'd always dreamed of marrying an architect. The rest, as they say, is history."

"The girl?" Laine asked, appalled at the knot in her stomach.

He chuckled. "I was already enrolled at Princeton when she decided she preferred football heroes to would-be architects." Murphy laughed, a full, rich sound. "I never even made a first down with her, though I imagine the quarterback did."

Laine relaxed, gazing out at their leafy enclosure. "I like your first effort. In some ways, it's probably still your favorite."

Murphy stretched out on his back, hands behind his head, knees bent. "I used to sleep out here when I was a teenager. I had this recurring fantasy that a beautiful woman would steal up the ladder at midnight, and teach me all the secrets of sex that I was bursting to know."

Laine swallowed. Somewhere along the way, he had learned all kinds of delectable secrets. Learned them well. "Did your fantasy woman ever appear?"

"No. But I still spend a night out here every so often." He propped himself up on one elbow and his hazel eyes bored into hers. There was more than friendship there. "Fantasies die hard, Laine."

9

EACH SUCCEEDING DAY brought another wave of relatives to Hilton Head for the wedding. And every day saw another series of small traumas that kept them in a continual state of turmoil. No matter how innocuous an opinion someone voiced, there was someone else waiting to dispute it. Then the rest felt it was their sacred obligation to take sides. By Wednesday, Laine had come to the conclusion that they just liked a good argument for the sake of it. They yelled and gestured at each other for hours, often straying far from the original subject of disagreement. She had never known a group of people that thrived on turbulence the way Murphy's family did.

The combat involved only Murphy's siblings and assorted relations from his mother's side, the Leblancs. Sybil had mentioned that no Murphy relative would get there until the wedding day. "Cerebral types," she confided to Laine. "They can't stand the bickering, even though it means nothing. It drives them mad." Laine had to admit that she was in complete agreement with the absent Murphys.

Through it all Colin remained the constant eye of the hurricane, the one who calmly resolved a never-ending procession of problems. They quarreled over everything—from the proper name for the color of the bridal attendants' dresses to who would ride with whom to the ceremony. When the caterer showed up with two samples of groom's cake, Laine expected them to come to blows over whether it should be light or dark chocolate. Murphy took the flustered lady aside and instructed her to make it a combination of both. The maid of honor broke her finger during a rowdy game of volleyball at a beach cookout. Murphy drove her to the emergency room.

Laine marveled at his patience and competence in handling this collection of basket cases. She wondered how they would have managed without his soothing presence. She also wondered when his uncharacteristic forbearance would end. Laine knew the petty, ceaseless discord was forcing Murphy into a role he was loath to play.

He grew quieter as the remainder of his family loudly approached the big day. His lazy smile and understated sense of humor vanished. Laine could almost see his mind withdrawing and his body growing visibly tauter. They were stretching his tolerance to the breaking point.

More than once she caught Murphy staring morosely at a blank sketch pad, his face a study in frustration. She yearned to comfort him, to tell him she understood. She wanted to spare him this anguish by acting as the buffer he claimed to need. But she hesitated to take that step, fearing that Murphy would interpret it as a sign of more than she intended.

At this point, Laine couldn't have stated for certain what her intentions were. The line between what she'd believed she wanted and what occupied most of her thoughts now was increasingly blurred.

Early Thursday morning Caroline, the bride to be, called to invite Laine to lunch. She and Josh's wife, Amy, had decided they needed a break from the tedium of wedding preparations. Laine agreed, wondering where they could go to lunch wearing bathing suits and shorts.

Shortly after eleven, the two women arrived with the top down on Caroline's yellow Volkswagen Rabbit convertible. Laine clambered in to share the backseat with a picnic basket. Driving the small car with a zest Laine admired, Caroline quickly piloted them to a remote stretch of sand. They removed an amazing collection of beach gear from the trunk, and staked their claim on a little spit of sand that extended out into the ocean. Amy positioned an umbrella to shade the food and cooler, then took out a corkscrew and a bottle of German wine.

As she accepted a wineglass, Laine saw two more bottles on ice and jokingly inquired, "Are we having a party, or what?"

"Definitely," Amy said, disposing of the cork and pouring each of them a generous portion. "I told my darling husband that baby Joshua is his responsibility until we wake up in the morning. Which ought to be interesting since tonight is Stephen's bachelor party."

"Can this island survive that much wildness?" Laine asked. "If they party with the same vigor that they argue and play, I hate to see the aftermath."

"Oh, we don't worry about things getting out of hand when Colin's with them," Amy said with a dismissing wave of her free hand. "He'll look out for everyone."

Just as he'd been acting as peacemaker all week, Laine reflected. Since they'd arrived in Hilton Head, she had seen a whole different side of Murphy. One that altered her opinion of him enough to make her doubt the wisdom of being here.

Even when she'd had him labeled as unsuitable, Laine had liked far too much about Colin Murphy. With each new insight into his depth of character, she became more captivated.

Amy raised her glass in a toast. "Long live the Outlaws. May we always hold on to our sense of humor, along with a tenuous grip on logic."

"Here, here," Caroline responded, clinking her glass with Amy's. Then she touched Laine's. "And welcome to our newest member."

Laine swallowed a tentative sip, feeling as though she had taken a first halting step into the unlikely alliance that Caroline and Amy seemed to be offering. She had the odd sensation of needing it, while at the same time being reluctant to embrace it fully.

It was the same kind of ambivalence she felt about Colin Murphy.

Amy misinterpreted her bemused look. "Don't get us wrong. We adore the Murphys. They're wonderful—generous and loving and loyal. It's just that nobody, not even a Murphy by marriage, can take a constant diet of them and their nonstop feuding. Thus, the Outlaws."

Laine smiled, remembering the conversation in her living room when Murphy was trying to convince her to come here with him. "Colin said pretty much the same thing. I think he feels slightly out of tune with his family. That's more or less why I'm here. I guess you can consider me an honorary Outlaw for the week."

Amy and Caroline exchanged glances, but it was Caroline who spoke. "Tell us that in a year," she said cryptically.

"Or a month," Amy chimed in.

Uncomfortable with their implications that she and Murphy had a future, Laine changed the subject. "Both of you seem to take the craziness in stride. How did you ever get used to it?" She noticed that Amy usually retained a calm air of detachment, and Caroline also stayed above the verbal fray.

"The secret is to keep them apart as much as possible," Caroline said mischievously. "It's only when they gather en masse that trouble erupts. Face it. They just love clashing over stuff that's totally unimportant. It's what they do for fun."

Laine shook her head, thinking how different that was from her family. Smokin' Joe did not allow arguing. Any complaints had to be presented logically and with a substitute plan of action. As ranking officer, he was the final authority.

Murphy was nothing like her father, yet he served the same function in family disagreements. "Colin is always the one to step in and resolve the problem."

"Or Neil, his father," Amy added. "Those two are the only cool heads when that troop gets together. Colin's been a real lifesaver since Neil started traveling so much. Who knows what would happen otherwise."

The three swam and sunbathed, sharing the picnic, a few confidences and a lot of laughter. Except when she was with Claire, Laine hadn't experienced this sort of female camaraderie in several years. Without consciously seeking it, she had slipped into a comfortable sisterhood with Amy and Caroline.

But she couldn't seem to chase away the picture that was forming of Colin as a loving and devoted family man. She tried to tell herself it had no relevance for her, that she didn't feel a little flicker of hope deep inside.

Because she was dangerously close to abandoning all her reservations, and letting her feelings determine her future.

Late that afternoon, Caroline and Amy dropped Laine back at the house after she'd agreed to join them later for a feminine version of the bachelor party. It would be, they promised her with foxy winks, a night to remember.

Everyone was gone so Laine ambled out to the deck and claimed a lounger facing the ocean. The soothing sound of waves surging onto the beach provided a serene counterpoint to the confusion that had swirled around her since she and Murphy had arrived.

Today had been fun and enlightening. Amy and Caroline had welcomed her without self-consciousness or restraint, just as the entire family had. As predicted, they all took it for granted that Laine and Murphy were romantically involved.

The sun's rays beat down and Laine squinted out beyond the frothy breakers. Murphy had stressed their friendship. But she didn't think men took women friends to visit their families in order to have a cover. Not men like Murphy, anyway. If his relatives didn't approve of him, that was their problem. He wouldn't change to please them.

So why was she here? She certainly couldn't accuse him of wanting convenient sex. He hadn't touched her all week, just as he'd promised. Aside from that brief interval in the tree house, he hadn't looked as if it were even on his mind. Of course, Murphy accomplished more with a quick look than any other man could with the most artful seduction.

Laine turned over on her stomach and closed her eyes. If that incredible night was truly a one-time phenomenon, why couldn't she obliterate it from her memory? It was never far from her awareness. Her physical feelings for Murphy were just as complicated, just as confusing as everything else about her attraction to him. But one fact was clear after being with him every day for almost three weeks. The attraction wasn't going to go away. Indeed it grew stronger every minute.

She had given up dwelling on the reasons why Murphy wasn't potential husband material. She'd already admitted that he had several of the traits she valued most. He was intelligent, imaginative, witty and successful. He treated her with consideration and apparently had no hang-ups about either her business success or her penchant for offbeat fun. But that still left the monumental obstacle of his instability. When Laine had decided to get married, she and Randy had had a long talk. They'd agreed that she would cut travel to a minimum and take over administrative responsibilities at R&R. She wanted her husband to be at home, and she wanted to be there with him.

Laine scrambled upright, stunned by the direction of her thoughts. She had made a hundred-and-eighty-degree shift. Now she was weighing the qualities in Murphy's favor, as if she *wanted* to marry him. She turned the revolutionary concept over and over in her mind, examining it from every angle. A shadow blocked out the sun, and Laine shaded her eyes, surprised to see Murphy.

His brother's baby son was asleep in a carrier and Murphy gripped the handle so tightly that Laine could see the bones in his hand. "Why don't we put Joshua over here," she suggested, taking the infant carrier and placing it in the shade of an umbrella table. Murphy wriggled his fingers and seemed to relax a bit.

"I figured baby-sitting was the one thing I'd be spared." He collapsed onto a lounger and massaged his neck as if he were exhausted. "What do I know about babies? I've never even held one."

Laine smiled at his injured tone. She hadn't had a lot of experience with babies either, but that didn't keep her from wanting several. She touched Joshua's tiny thumb and his fingers reflexively closed over hers. "I think you learn by doing."

"But they're so small. Noisy. Demanding. And something nasty is always coming out of one end or the other. Why would you, uh, anyone, knowingly undertake something so overwhelming?"

"I guess you do it out of love," she tossed back, attempting a cheerfulness she was far from feeling. Laine rebuked herself. She shouldn't be surprised that Murphy was no more interested in parenthood than he was in marriage. But hearing it confirmed shouldn't be this depressing. "Everyone in your family seems to think this little guy is worth the effort."

"Ah, yes," he said, jumping up to stalk the deck's perimeter. "What you have to understand is that Murphys are into procreating. Since I didn't contribute my quota, the pressure was really on Josh. I suppose Stephen will be feeling the heat soon."

The smile Laine had been directing at Joshua dissolved into a little frown. Murphy stopped his pacing and came to sit across from her at the table. "I'm sorry to have dragged you into all this. I should have known the insanity would be worse than usual. My only excuse is that I haven't been back for a while, and never just prior to one of the weddings."

"It was something of a shock in the beginning, but I got over that after the first couple of days. Now I'm almost used to it." She told him about her day with Amy and Caroline. "They both had high praise for you as the family diplomat."

"I guess I'm the logical successor when Dad can't do it. He and I have always been alike in that we're sort of moody and introspective. We need to be by ourselves, and believe it or not, everybody else respects that and leaves us alone most of the time. Individually each of them is decent enough. It's just when they have a cause to rally around, or fight about, that things turn manic. Then Dad or I intervene."

After a long silence, he said, "Who knows why, but the same rules don't apply to families as to everyone else. We let them manipulate us in ways that we'd never allow an outsider."

He wasn't looking at her, but Laine felt as if he were probing deeply. She didn't reply, but yes, she knew that it was difficult to escape family demands. Even though The General wasn't an ideal father, she never gave up trying to please him. And recently she had recognized that Maureen's suicide was still hanging over her, influencing her future. An admission she'd swept under the rug for too long. It was time to resolve it.

The baby squirmed and began to fret, fighting the intrusion of waking. His fussiness quickly escalated into a full-blown squall. The kid had great lungs.

"Like I said. Noisy." Murphy watched Laine pick Joshua up and arrange him on her lap, facing her. When she began to sing softly in French—a legacy from her French baby-sitter, he guessed—Murphy came around the table to look over her shoulder. The effect was instantaneous. Joshua stopped crying after the first few words.

Murphy was amazed. He pulled up a low stool and sank onto it, continuing to study the baby's abrupt change of expression. Laine sang another verse, and slowly, Joshua's eyes opened. Murphy eyes. But instead of focusing in the direction of the gentling voice, he looked directly at his uncle. And then he smiled.

That smile hit Murphy like a karate kick to the chest. He blinked and swallowed at the same time, not quite sure how to handle the sudden rush of strange emotions. For the first time ever, he could almost identify with the intense pride and protectiveness a man would feel if he had helped create such a perfectly formed little person. The love and loyalty he'd feel toward the woman who'd helped in that creation.

"Now, Uncle Colin," Laine said triumphantly, "I defy anyone to resist a charmer who looks at you with eyes like that."

Murphy looked at Laine—with eyes like that—and hoped her challenge was prophetic.

FOR AN EVENT doomed to be a disaster, the wedding went off without a glitch. The bride was radiantly beautiful; her groom, proudly handsome. The candle-lit church sanctuary, adorned with exotic blossoms, formed a lovely backdrop for the moving words of love and commitment.

But Laine's breath caught when Murphy took his place beside his brother at the altar. She hadn't seen him in those final frenzied hours of the afternoon. The transformation was stunning. With his hair expertly trimmed, wearing a tuxedo that might have been custom-tailored to his lithe body, he looked almost handsome. No, she needn't qualify it. He looked handsome.

Earlier that day, when Neil Murphy had at last made an appearance, Laine came face-to-face with the source of Colin's magnificent eyes. As an increasing crowd of Murphys showed up in the chaotic household, she saw the trait repeated over and over. There didn't seem to be any end to the number of attractive cousins. Neil was the eldest of six boys, all of whom exhibited the same tendency to sire good-looking male offspring. In quantity. Any woman who was susceptible to eyes that sizzled with bone-melting sensuality had better be on guard against such prolific masculinity.

Laine was unmoved by every one of them except Colin. Giving herself a mental jolt, she turned her attention to the exchange of vows. By the time Stephen had kissed Caroline and the organ music had swelled, she was misty-eyed with an emotion that was as foreign as it was powerful.

She had fallen hopelessly in love with Colin Murphy.

Realizing it was the easy part. Dealing with how it would affect her life wouldn't be quite so simple. But that would have to wait until some other time. A reception was to immediately follow the ceremony and there would be friends and relatives surrounding her and Murphy every minute. Later the house would no doubt be full of them, too. Except for a few brief times, Laine and Murphy had not been alone since they'd hit the island.

It was both a blessing and a curse.

The reception, held in one of the local beach clubs, was as tastefully subdued as the wedding itself. Laine had always found the South's adherence to customs and etiquette quaintly charming. It was so much more gracious and refined than the military protocol that she had been raised on.

She worked her way through the reception line, shaking hands, saying the proper things. Until she congratulated the groom, spoke to the maid of honor and felt Murphy's warm hand enclose hers and his breath whisper against her ear.

"The dress is beautiful, Sunshine."

She was about to thank him for the compliment when he added, "What you *weren't* wearing a week ago did a lot more for me."

Laine knew she was blushing above her discreetly daring neckline, but she smiled and ground her foot into the toe of his shiny shoes. "How ungentlemanly of you, Murphy. Just when I was going to say how handsome you look in full dress."

His eyes blazed, one finger skipped along her palm. Without a word he reminded her of how easily he'd swept her away without the trappings of formal clothing. Laine glanced down at their entwined hands, then met his gaze. She not only loved and respected him, she wanted to be near him always. Women with much less in their favor had taken greater risks. Was she courageous enough to do the same?

Before her vacation was over, Laine knew she'd have the answer. Her future depended on it.

Murphy accepted another limp handshake, and watched Laine melt into the crowd. He'd seen wariness, indecision and determination when their eyes met. Things were coming to a head. All week her outward disposition had been as sunny as usual, but beneath it all he sensed that she was confronting private demons. He couldn't shake the awful premonition that she was going to bolt, knowing he would have to let her go. If only for a short time.

He'd wanted to give her some room, but he was tired of concealing his true feelings for her. A few shockingly primitive male instincts had interfered. He wanted to claim his mate so that she, and everyone else, knew Laine belonged to him. But apparently a whole pack of his male relatives had failed to get the message. Satisfied that he'd done his duty, Murphy left the reception line.

He watched the festivities from behind the cover of a potted plant, much as he had the day he'd first met Laine. His cousins were brazenly plying her with champagne and food. Did they expect to reap some corresponding reward? Murphy could tell them that Laine wasn't impressed by the obvious.

"I suppose a woman who's shopping for a husband might find a lot of prime material right here," he said, creeping up behind her.

"I was thinking the same thing myself."

"Blaine's a body builder," Murphy said, shamelessly sabotaging the cousin he liked most. "Palpitating pectorals and quivering quadriceps. Mutant muscles."

She cast him a sidelong glance and made a face. "Disgusting."

"Umm. And Grant is a renegade. Had to be sent off to military school when he was twelve. It did the trick for his rebelliousness, but they say he still miters his bed sheets."

The corners of Laine's mouth twitched temptingly. "He really ought to explore the pleasures of wallowing. In his bed sheets."

"Amen," Murphy said, dragging his eyes from her cleavage to survey the crowd for more victims. "I don't guess Robert told you his middle name is Dennis," he speculated innocently. "But you probably noticed the little gold stud in his ear. That's almost as bad as a pinky ring. Maybe worse."

"Murphy, does this conversation seem absurdly reminiscent?"

"Absurdly."

"You've made your point." The idea that Murphy might feel a bit possessive of her secretly thrilled Laine. It also worried her. Surely she couldn't find that trait appealing. She motioned to Caroline and Stephen who were waltzing. "It would be a shame if someone else asked me to dance before you did."

"Point taken," he said, slipping his arms around her for the first time in what seemed like an eternity.

AFTER THE RECEPTION a large number of the entourage returned to Sybil and Neil's house. Murphys and Leblancs alike were in high spirits, eager to cling to the evening's magic. They relived every minute, especially the incident when the five-year-old ring bearer demanded, "Where's Colin?" just as he reached the end of the aisle.

"I'm sure he didn't recognize you in your tux," one of the aunts told Murphy. "After all, he was barely born the last time you dressed up. That was for Josh's wedding. And he's already a father," she tacked on for emphasis.

Laine watched Murphy swallow a retort. His chest rose and fell rapidly from the effort. As attention increasingly centered on him, she could almost feel the resentment pulsing through him. He was about to climb the walls.

When their conversation turned to the subject of marriage—his—the consensus was that if he didn't hurry, Erica, the last of his younger siblings, would beat him to the altar. He stood abruptly, shot a venomous glare at the crowd in general and stormed from the room, taking the stairs two at a time.

"What's gotten into him?"

Murphy's father came to his defense. "He's had a hard week trying to hold everything together. I couldn't get out of translating for that foreign-trade delegation to Japan. Colin had to take over for me and keep the various elements from falling apart at the last minute. His mother tells me there were an unusual number of fires to put out." He smiled wryly, as if he recognized an understatement when he heard it. "I think my oldest son has just reached the end of his rope."

If any reinforcement was needed, Murphy provided it. He'd only been gone a few minutes when he came thundering back down the stairs. He paused in the doorway of the huge party room just long enough for everyone to see that he'd discarded the tuxedo in favor of red jogging shorts and deck shoes. Tucked under his arm was a rolled-up sleeping bag. A towel hung from one shoulder.

Laine tried, but couldn't keep her gaze disinterested. Earlier he had looked so handsome in the tuxedo. In abbreviated shorts, his chest and legs bare, his near nudity conjured up visions that had teased her all week. His eyes met hers for an instant and her heart started to race. For days, Murphy had played the civilized negotiator, the polite gentleman. Tonight the barriers were down.

Without a word, he vanished toward the back of the house.

"Well, that's the last we'll see of old Colin tonight," one of his cousins said. "He's off to his woodsy hideout." He looked at Laine so knowingly that for a few seconds she was afraid she'd confessed her intentions aloud.

She stayed a while longer for appearances' sake, then made the socially correct excuses to her hosts. Knowing what she was going to do, Laine didn't waste time vindicating her decision. She was in love, and Murphy needed her to prove it in the most basic way any woman can. For now she could suspend her doubts about the future and give him something he'd always wanted.

She discarded the striking blue silk in favor of a white satin teddy under a sheer gauze dress that skimmed her curves and shifted sensuously against her skin. The sophisticated hairstyle fell victim to her brush and her shoes were left behind. Heart pounding, almost breathless with anticipation, Laine took time to dab perfume at her throat and on her wrists.

After stealing down the back stairs she made her way through the beachside courtyard toward the bower where Murphy's tree house was hidden. Beyond the range of indirect lighting, she had to depend on the pale light of a half-moon, fitfully obstructed by fast-moving clouds. There was no indication that anyone was around, but with the special perception unique to lovers, Laine could feel Murphy's nearness.

The surf's measured roll blended into hushed sounds of the woods at night, creating a haven alive with expectancy. Confidently, knowing she was doing the right thing, Laine began to scale the ladder.

She'd only gotten midway up when Murphy said, "Go away, Sunshine. This is off limits, remember?"

She halted, drawing a quiet breath before climbing the last three steps. "Not to me."

"*Especially* to you, tonight. I'm pretty well used up."

"I know. That's why I'm here."

10

As SHE PAUSED in the shadows, Laine's blood was singing, as if champagne had been injected into her veins. Never had she done anything this impetuous, this daring. This important.

"Your fantasy lover, Colin . . . did she talk?"

"She—" Laine heard him swallow. "She whispered."

"Like this?"

"Yesss," he breathed, matching her soft sounds.

She took a step forward, the brush of her bare feet over the smooth wood planking nearly inaudible. "What did she wear?"

"Something white . . . sort of swirling and—"

"See through?" Laine moved in front of the window so her outline was visible against the slice of moonlight streaming through the trees. She wove her fingers into her unbound hair, her breasts thrusting against the filmy fabric.

The color of his eyes was obscured by the pale illumination. But the appreciative glimmer was not. "Sunshine," Murphy groaned. "You're not playing fair."

She swayed sinuously, allowing the silvered light to filter through the gauze. "There are no rules in a fantasy, Colin. Anything you want will happen." Laine stepped closer. Even without touching, she felt the heat and leashed vitality of him engulfing her.

He was on his back, naked, unable to conceal the reaction that her midnight appearance had inspired. Murphy came up on one elbow and groped for his towel. But she bent down and stopped him from covering himself by grasping his wrist and casting the towel aside with her other hand. "No secrets allowed. We don't need them where we're going."

Laine rubbed her lips over the back of his hand, his palm. "You've been in the ocean."

"I had to. I need—"

"I know what you need. I'll give it to you. Just . . . not . . . too . . . fast," she whispered, punctuating her words by licking the salty traces from each of his fingers.

"You're killing me."

She laughed softly. "Not yet, Colin. But soon. Soon."

He laughed, too, the shaky sound interrupted when she stood again and drew up the hem of her transparent dress. With a languid motion she pulled it over her head and knelt beside him, trailing it over his chest, his arms, his legs, absorbing the drops he had missed with the towel.

Heat from his skin penetrated the thin fabric, warming her fingers as they glided over muscles that flexed and bunched under the delicate pressure.

Murphy's hand clamped over her shoulder as if he needed proof that she was real. Fingers spread, the hand traced the valley between her breasts, over the slope of her hip, stopping only to toy with the lace that hemmed the high-cut legs of her teddy.

Laine pinned both his hands at his sides and bent to moisten the curve of his ear with her tongue. She felt tremors shoot through him when her breath fanned the damp skin. "Did your fantasy woman touch you here?"

Her mouth washed over the small, tight buds nestled in the musky dampness on his chest. His only answer was a low, hungry sound.

"Here?" Her teeth left tiny tracks down the center of his body until she reached the dip of his navel and discovered that the stroke of her tongue caused his torso to undulate with waves of pleasure.

"Ah, Lord, Laine. I'm warning you. I can't take much more of this."

He strained against the supple manacles that kept him from touching her, and at last Laine freed him. Shaping herself to him she flowed slowly over his length, letting the satin shimmer between them, blending smooth with rough, cool with warmth, until there was nothing but heat and sensation and a promise of ecstasy so intense it was close to pain.

Her tongue flicked at his lips, urging them to part for her. His taste, familiar and yet as exciting as it had been at the beginning, almost made her forget why she'd come to his retreat. She pulled her mouth away and slid down his body, using her hands to arouse him further. Laine was driven by an overwhelming need to give. To soothe his depression, ease his tension. Fulfill his fantasy.

"Laine, don't. I'm not in control. I'll— Oh, God!" His voice shattered in a hoarse cry for mercy.

"Shh," she murmured, feeling invincible because she could do this to him. For him. "I can't teach you anything about sex. Let me show you something even more magical." *Let me prove my love the only way I can tonight.*

"It's what I want." Her mouth moved over him, hot and wet. Her own pleasure was not a consideration. She didn't think of it, didn't need it.

When Murphy let go of his pent-up emotion, it was channeled into a reckless, driving passion. Living his fantasy made him a little wild, a little rough. He uttered curses, prayers. Pleas.

Until Laine released the two snaps of her teddy and eased over him. Inside her at last, he couldn't speak at all. The only sounds were of desire, raw and urgent, and finally, a shout of surrender, muted against her shoulder.

He lay still, shaking, arms at his sides. Laine was draped over him, the moisture from their joint exertions binding them together. When the night slipped back into focus, she reluctantly began separating herself from him, and he let her.

"Laine, you should have listened to me," he said, his voice shaded by awe and gratitude and remorse. "I couldn't—" He sucked in a ragged breath. "I gave you nothing—"

You gave me everything that you are. Everything that I love. "Sometimes that's what it's all about, Murphy."

His golden eyes were unreadable in the shadows, but she felt him relax slightly, as if he knew what she meant.

"I love you, you know."

He had never sounded so serious, and Laine didn't doubt his words. "Yes, I think I realized that when I stopped fabricating reasons why it couldn't happen."

His entire body went rigid in defiance of the powerful release that had just rocked him. "But you're leaving anyway, aren't you?"

She touched his shoulder, an unspoken bid for understanding. "I'm not ready to accept what falling in love means. I have to get some things straight in my head before I can say the words."

"But you do—"

Laine grasped his hand and laid his fingers against her lips while she said the words in a fervent, silent appeal. *I love you, Colin Murphy, but please be patient.*

She felt his head nod in acceptance. "Then come here," he said, stripping off the teddy and lowering her onto her back. "This time I'll give you something to take with you."

He was neither subtle nor gentle in his determination to draw out every feminine response, every wanton cry Laine was capable of giving. She relinquished them all. But he demanded more.

"I'll make sure you don't forget this night, Sunshine. And I will *never* let you forget me."

WHEN LAINE HEADED NORTH at dawn, it felt as if she were completing the final leg of a three-week, three-state odyssey. She'd left Atlanta for the North Carolina mountains exactly three weeks ago. Today she was going back to where it all began—to figure out how it was going to end.

She didn't know why, but it was essential to recreate her meeting with Murphy, and those initial feelings of attraction. She hadn't known at the time, but she must have started to fall in love with Colin Murphy from the first word he'd said to her. She even remembered it. "Philistines," he'd sympathized, tongue in cheek, when nobody at the seminar would comment on her amateurishly carved piglet. She ought to have recognized a kindred spirit right away. But while she'd been busy adding up Murphy's negatives on one side, his treacherous appeal had crept up on her from the other. By the time she'd gotten wise, it was too late.

Now the situation was far more critical than conquering an unsuitable attraction. What did an intelligent woman do when she was desperately in love, and desperately frightened of committing herself totally?

The knowledge that she had met the challenge by skipping out made Laine floor the accelerator. The Corvette streaked forward with a savage growl. She had always envisioned herself as a person who met problems head-on. But from this, perhaps the most important decision of her life, she'd run.

She owed Murphy more than a cowardly defection. Laine hoped she could conquer her reservations and give him what he deserved.

She burned up the interstate highways, giving her car its head. Speed limit be damned. This wasn't the time to meander through the countryside. She had to reach her destination so she could begin to work through the ambivalence that had dogged her for three weeks. Laine knew she wouldn't rest until she'd decided on a course of action.

She had no trouble getting a room at the mountain resort. For the next two days she did nothing but prowl the woods and walk the grounds, lingering in all the spots that reminded her of something she'd shared with Murphy. Each recollection served to further interweave him into the fabric of her life. Every memory solidified her love. And one certainty emerged, dominating all others.

Her present fears were nothing when balanced against a future without Murphy.

Laine spent one more day in solitary soul-searching. Forcing herself to be brutally honest, she confronted the reasons she was afraid to risk everything and make a complete commitment to one man. Her conclusions were both revealing and unsettling. She wondered how she'd been able to ignore them so adroitly for two years. But at least now she knew what she had to overcome.

"The most crucial current goal in my life plan," Laine quoted Amanda. Apparently she'd learned her lessons well during the short seminar. Because now she not only knew what that goal was, she'd defined the obstacles blocking her from attaining it. Best of all, she knew what to do to remove those obstacles.

But before putting her plan into operation, she needed a sounding board. As she'd been doing for nearly twenty years, Laine automatically thought of

Claire. It had to be fate that her best friend lived so close. She could get there in less than two hours.

It was closer to three hours before she spied the number on Claire's mailbox. Several roadside stops had proven irresistible. Laine couldn't wait to present Murphy with his own Elvis on black velvet.

Claire had said their three acres had lots of trees. She'd neglected to mention that they had carved their homestead out of the woods. In first gear Laine followed the gently sloping drive until she saw the one-story brick conforming to the crest of a small hill.

Anxious to see Claire for the first time in months, Laine abandoned her luggage in the driveway and hurried up the walk. Her finger was poised over the button when the door was swept open. The two women hugged in that special way reserved for longtime friends and Laine stepped inside, letting the coolness wash over her. It seemed twenty degrees warmer here than in the mountains.

"Honestly, Claire," she said, rearranging her windswept hair as she followed her friend into an enormous high-ceilinged family room. "For a while I was worried that you'd have to send a search party out to rescue me. I was positive I was lost, and stopped for directions. Naturally the guy had never heard of this place. I should have remembered that the first job requirement for gas-station attendants is total lack of knowledge regarding directions."

Without stopping, Laine rushed to the wall of glass that looked out over a narrow backyard and more woods. "It's so quiet and peaceful here. But I'd never have pictured you in such a pastoral setting." She turned to face Claire with a gleam of devilment in her eye. "Remember when we were thirteen and marooned outside of Minot, North Dakota? You swore you were going to spend the rest of your life amid the bright glaring neon lights."

Claire chuckled at the reminder. "I also said I was never going to get married and have babies. So what did I do?" She walked over to an antique wicker bassinet and lifted a small yellow-swathed bundle. "Got pregnant on my honeymoon. What can you say about a modern woman who does something like that?"

Laine smiled at the look of maternal devotion Claire bestowed on her daughter. "Creativity, not math, was always your strong suit. You probably slipped up when you counted the days on your calendar." That earned a hearty guffaw.

"Since when did you become so diplomatic? Bluntness was always more your style." Claire came forward, holding the baby so Laine could see her. "Laura Elaine, meet your godmother."

For the second time within a week, Laine held a baby in her arms. Weddings, honeymoons, babies—suddenly she was besieged with them. She took it as an omen that she'd made the right decision. Not that she was superstitious, but a little extra assurance never did any harm. Wasn't that why she'd come here?

"Hello, precious," she crooned when the newly awake infant regarded her out of solemn blue eyes fringed with ridiculously long dark lashes. "Aren't you a beauty? You'll have the guys standing in line."

"Please," Claire said laughingly. "She's less than three months old and already her father is talking about getting a shotgun."

Laine joined the laughter, but could tell that Claire was half-serious. With sons, parents might feel a certain amount of tolerance where the opposite sex was concerned. While she didn't have one, Laine understood that daughters were an entirely different matter. They had to be protected from the rakes of this world. In his own gruff way, even Smokin' Joe had gotten that message across to his little girls.

Laine envisioned Murphy meeting The General, and smiled. Now there was an interesting prospect.

"Come into the kitchen," Claire said. "I'll fix us something cold to drink. You must be hot and tired from the trip."

"Yes, I could use—" She stopped in her tracks. "Claire, you've got weeds and noodles all over your kitchen counters." With one arm still holding Laura, the other gestured at an endless array of herbs, spices and pasta, all displayed in glass containers. "I can't believe you've turned into a pasta gourmand."

She spent a few minutes lamenting the radical alteration in Claire's life-style, eating habits, even the car she drove.

"Laine," Claire said gravely, pausing in the act of removing crushed ice from the refrigerator door. "If— notice I said *if*, not when—you get married, I'll give you a year. Then I'm going to show up and gloat over all the changes you've undergone during that time." She filled two glasses from a pitcher of tea. "Let's go out on the deck and sit in the shade. You can tell me all about the reason you're over a week late getting here."

They took a quick tour through the house, ending up in the sun room off the master bedroom. In here, Claire had used her tacky treasures sparingly, most likely in deference to her husband. But there were enough tasteless objects scattered around to give the room flavor. The gift Laine had picked up on the way, a florid oil painting pretentiously titled *Nice, France, by Night*, would be a perfect addition.

Double French doors opened onto a deck that jutted out over a small creek that bisected the property. When they were seated, Claire said, "Now about this friend who invited you to the wedding in Hilton Head. Anyone I know?"

Laine had been deliberately vague when she'd called Claire about her delayed arrival. At that time, she'd been clinging to the false assumption that she could spend just a while longer with Murphy and still walk away.

Now it was time to level with her friend. She supplied all the details about her meeting with Murphy and everything that had followed, including her dramatic discovery that she'd fallen in love with him.

Laine hesitated, taking a few sips while studying the hickory and dogwood trees that formed most of the woods on the opposite side of the creek. "You see, Murphy isn't the type I'd pictured myself marrying. Nor did the relationship develop as I'd expected."

She looked at Claire and plodded ahead. "I said right away that he wasn't viable husband material, then proceeded to spend practically every waking minute with him. To make matters worse, we ended up going to bed after knowing each other less than two weeks."

Claire let out a surprised whistle. "That must have shaken you up pretty good. You've never done anything that impulsive with a man before."

"Exactly. Intense passion was not a requirement. Actually I figured I was immune to the kind of passion that takes you completely outside yourself." Murphy had used that description and it was an appropriate one. Apparently he'd believed himself to be just as immune as she had.

"So it's not what you expected," Claire reflected. "That's not the world's most insoluble problem. Thinking you have any control over whether you fall in love, or when or with whom is one of life's greatest myths. I'm a perfect example. Twelve months ago my bags were as good as packed for a two-year photography assignment in Europe. Look at me now. Husband, baby and three acres on the edge of nowhere."

"But you must resent it," Laine protested, her chest tightening with anxiety. "Don't you regret giving up everything, having someone else control your life, taking the ultimate risk because you fell in love with a man who taught you about passion?"

Claire frowned. "Just wait a minute here, friend. I must have missed some vital link in this conversation. What are you talking about—giving up everything, losing yourself and taking the ultimate risk?"

She didn't give Laine a chance to answer. "Sure I gave up some things. So did Ted. But, don't you see? That's what love means. Caring about someone, knowing that they care for you in return, more than compensates for what you lost." Claire looked Laine right in the eye. "There is no assignment in this world that could take the place of being with my husband and baby."

"But what if something happens to him?" Laine demanded starkly. "What if he leaves you, or dies?" The next words stuck in her throat like a bitter pill, but she had to say them. "What if he gets killed and you can't go on living?"

"Of course I— Oh, God, Laine. It's Maureen, isn't it?" Claire's voice dropped to a whisper. "What happened to her is why you're afraid to risk love and marriage to Colin Murphy. You're terrified you'll end up like your sister."

Laine wasn't accustomed to emotional turmoil. When blue moods overtook her, she fought them. She wanted to jump up and challenge Claire to do something impetuous and silly. Instead she didn't move a muscle. Finally she admitted, "You're half-right. I am terrified. It's probably irrational, but a great deal of life is. Anyway my mind is made up. I've decided to take the chance. Cross your fingers, light candles or whatever else you can think of that might help." Laine thought she struck just the right note of perkiness. Until Claire took her hand.

"Laine, we've never talked about this, even though I know we should have. But both your parents cursed you with stoic genes. Stiff upper lip, the show must go on and all that rot."

Laine strained to laugh at her friend's too-apt description. She was rewarded with a scowl and a, "See what I mean." She sobered at once.

"Have you ever cried for Maureen, Laine?" Claire inquired seriously. "For what she was? And what she wasn't. Because that's what made her do what she did. Not falling in love with Jeff. Not because she tasted passion. Not because he died."

Laine jumped up and planted both hands on the deck rail. Knowing what Claire was hinting at didn't make it any easier to face. But it had been there all along, even when they were children. "Maureen glorified perfection. Failure at anything she attempted was unthinkable, intolerable. So she never tried anything unless she was absolutely certain she'd succeed." Laine turned to look at Claire with a dawning realization. "She was obsessed, wasn't she? And sometime, in some way, she was doomed to fail. The tragedy is that she couldn't cope with it."

"She wasn't you, Laine. Never had been. Never could be. And you're not her. That's why you should mourn for her, then put it behind you. Your life has taken off in a new direction, and I think you'd better hurry and catch up with it. You don't need crossed fingers or candles. But I will give you a hug for good luck."

Laine felt her eyes cloud with tears; her throat ached. "Oh, damn! I hate being emotional. It's so messy and it never solves anything."

"Sweetie, I hate to tell you, but you may as well get in practice. Pregnancy is nine months of crying over nothing."

Laine took a walk in the woods while Claire fed Laura. She had so much to think about, and yet everything was in perspective at last. She could go to Murphy confident that she was free from the same insecurities that had hounded Maureen. And she could get married without the specter of dire consequences that might befall her.

She congratulated herself for arriving at two such momentous conclusions. Until it occurred to her that she now had two equally momentous problems. First, she didn't know where to find Murphy. Second, and even more daunting, he'd said he loved her. Which didn't necessarily mean that he was panting to get married. What if she'd finally accepted that marriage to Murphy was what she really wanted, only to find that his perception of love was radically different from hers?

Suppose he was thinking in terms of a long-distance liaison? The kind where he'd fly into Atlanta once a month or so, indulge in a few days of wild lovemaking, then jet off into the sunset until next time. Well, she'd straighten him out about that. Laine Randolph knew about setting a goal. And Colin Murphy knew what hers was. If he was offering anything less than a gold band, he'd have to look elsewhere. She'd set him straight about that in no uncertain terms. First chance she got.

Later that evening, Laine was in her room, emptying her suitcase so she could repack. She'd been hasty and careless when she'd fled Hilton Head. When she left here in the morning—wherever she was headed—her clothes would be laundered and neatly packed. She got to the bottom layer of the bag, and beneath the shoes she found an envelope.

That single word lettered on the outside made her eyes fill again. Two bouts of tears in one day was simply too much. But she pressed the envelope to her heart before opening it. It was addressed to *Sunshine*. Inside it read:

Laine,
When you're ready, this is where you can find me.
I'll be waiting.

Love,
Colin

His writing was precise and legible. It almost made up for the arrogant message. If she hadn't skipped down to the postscript, Laine might have been tempted to toss the whole thing in a convenient wastebasket. It said:

P.S. This map is good for one week only. After that, I'll be gone—coming after you.

JCM

Laine loved him madly, couldn't wait to marry him, but she had no idea what the *J* stood for. How could she possibly have decided to pledge her future to a man whose full name she didn't know? It didn't make sense.

But of course, love wasn't meant to make sense. Defying rationality, it existed in its own special realm. You loved in spite of reason, not because of it. That was the true test.

She wondered if Murphy had any idea how hard it was for an engineer to accept such an unnatural, impractical concept. She'd be sure to tell him that, too, when she delivered her ultimatum for marriage.

Laine hoped it wouldn't take all day tomorrow to reach Murphy. Now that she'd made up her mind, she was eager to get on with it. She turned the note over to examine the detailed map and directions for the first time. At her first brief glance, the paper fluttered to the floor. Scrambling around on her hands and knees to retrieve it, she wondered aloud, "What are you up to this time, Murphy?"

Her forehead wrinkled when she studied the drawing. He couldn't . . . no, it wasn't possible.

THE CORVETTE IDLED while Laine massaged her shoulder muscle and squinted at the open gate. She'd been driving hard since early morning to get here, but had begun to suspect that Murphy was leading her on a merry chase with this map. There hadn't been any sign of habitation for the past fifteen minutes. Maybe he was punishing her for running out on him. No, she was definitely in the right place. A description of the gate right in front of her was the last thing in his directions.

He had omitted that the gate led onto a narrow causeway which in turn connected to a tiny island a few hundred yards out in the Atlantic. A private island from all indications. Murphy's. As she drove forward, excitement rippled through Laine. Nothing about her man was conventional. Why should he live like anyone else?

Dramatically beautiful in its solitude, his house was surrounded by sea oats-covered dunes. It looked like no other house she had ever seen. Raised on wood pilings, its weathered cedar shingles contrasted with bands of white trim. The simplest way she could think to describe it was as an isosceles triangle with a cupola on top.

Latticework concealed the ground level except for two parking spaces. One side sheltered a disreputable Jeep, the other a sleek, dark green Jaguar sedan. One of Murphy's creature comforts, she guessed.

Like the gate, the front door stood ajar, as if someone were expecting her. Laine stepped inside and immediately caught the ocean breeze that funneled in through a wall of doors and uniquely shaped windows. She was aware of a remarkable sense of light and space in the open living area, could see beyond it to a screened porch. But she wasn't here to admire the architecture. Yet.

She'd come for the architect.

A quick reconnaissance of the main floor didn't turn up her quarry so Laine scaled the pickled-oak stairs. More odd-shaped windows followed the stairwell upward, each providing a view of the Atlantic. The next level consisted of a spacious hall, two bedrooms and a bath. But no Murphy.

Intrigued, her fingers closed around the teak ship's ladder, which climbed to the cupola. That's where she would find him. Laine had built-in radar when Murphy was anywhere near.

The room boasted a three-hundred-and-sixty-degree view. Even if he hadn't been here, she'd know that this was where he worked. Murphy sat in a canvas director's chair, facing east, with the afternoon sun at his back. Dressed only in swim trunks, he was making swift, decisive strokes on the sketch pad in his lap. With stereo earphones hugging his head, he was in another world.

Laine pulled the plug from the headphone jack, shutting off whatever he'd been listening to. The pencil skittered to the floor; Murphy swung around, primed for combat. She made a mental note never to disturb him that way again.

"Sunshine." That one word, and the way he looked at her held surprise, relief, hope. The sketch pad sailed off to one side, his earphones to the other and he came out of the chair in a smooth, continuous motion. "If you're here for any reason other than the obvious, don't tell me. I've come up with some pretty spectacular fantasies about this cupola, too." He came toward her in a slow stalk.

Laine knew that once he started kissing her she'd forget every word of the speech she'd been rehearsing all day. She hurried to get out the most important part, figuring the rest could wait until later. "Colin Murphy—I'd say your whole name if I knew what the *J* stands for—I love you. I want to marry you." She reached for his hand, unable to last another second without touching him. "And without much effort, you could probably convince me to stay here on your island forever."

"John," he said, supplying the unknown name. His hands gently framed her face. "Sunshine, I'm not greedy. All I want is you. With me. The island—and everything else—is negotiable."

Everything, perhaps, but his need to kiss her, Laine thought distractedly. If the frenzied way his lips moved over hers was any indication, nothing could have stopped him from claiming that.

The sensuous slide of his tongue caressing hers in an intimate rhythm sent heat coursing through Laine, settling deep in the pit of her stomach. She wrapped her arms around Murphy, melting against him, needing only to feel a sense of oneness with him.

There had never been another person, not Maureen, not Claire, certainly no man, with whom she wanted to share a unity of hearts and souls as she did with Murphy.

Because she wanted to be completely honest with him from this point, Laine knew she had to explain everything. She would tell him why she had run, and why she was now able to come to him unencumbered and free to love.

Grudgingly she broke the contact and took a deep breath. "I have to explain why I left. You need to understand."

"Sunshine," he said bringing her back into the circle of his arms, "your being here says all I need to know." His mouth found her collarbone and began to nibble.

"But aren't you— Oh!" Laine trembled against him. "Murphy, I can't think with your tongue in my ear."

With uncharacteristic speed and obedience, he abandoned her ear. "You like it better here?"

Like was too tame a word for the flames of passion that he ignited in her. "You're licking my neck," she accused huskily.

"Mmm. I'm working my way down."

In unison, the straps of Laine's sundress slipped down her arms, and his tongue lingered teasingly at the hollow of her throat. "Murphy, stop! I've got to do this now."

"And I've got to do *this*. Now."

Laine heard the faint clicks as he slowly rolled the zipper down her back. Her dress was losing the battle and so was she.

She was bare to the waist now, and Murphy's hands massaging her back, his chest rubbing against her nipples sparked such a feverish yearning that she forgot what had been important only seconds ago. How could oxygen be this scarce at sea level?

"God, Laine, I'm not letting you go again. Ever."

And she never wanted to go. But first . . . "Please. I want to tell you everything."

"Later," he whispered. "You can tell me anything you want to then. Right now, darlin', I'm not in any condition to listen." His hands worked lower to shape the yielding softness of her, then lifted her against him. "See?"

No, but she could feel. He lowered her with aching slowness, moaning when Laine thrust her hips against the straining hardness that fit her so perfectly. She wasn't sure whose hands were more eager, but between them, her dress floated to the floor and his shorts followed quickly.

Murphy's hand framed the back of Laine's neck, the other slipped inside the final barrier between him and the sweet, silken center of her desire. "You've missed me, too," he whispered, one finger gliding through the warm, moist proof of his claim.

In Hilton Head Laine had tried to communicate her feelings with her body. Now that she was free to use the words, too, she'd found a heady combination. "Colin, love me."

"I do, Sunshine. I will."

"Here?"

"Yes! I can't wait."

Laine gasped as his tongue filled her mouth. When she reciprocated eagerly, he buried himself with exquisite care in the smooth velvet of her.

She was home at last.

Locked together, moving as one, they soared to a pinnacle of desire and need and love. And for once, Laine was not ashamed of the joyful tears that fell onto Colin Murphy's face.

"GUESS I'M GREEDIER than I thought."

Laine sighed contentedly and wrapped her arms around Murphy. She didn't want even the slightest distance between them. The second time they'd made love had been as gentle and unhurried as the first had been fast and urgent. They had come down to the main level and Laine was about to reopen the issue of her defection. But Murphy had got that look in his eyes again and the next thing she knew, he'd carried her off to the master bedroom.

"You have a suspiciously healthy appetite for a man who claims to have no trouble staying celibate."

"Have pity. I'm a weakened man. This is not the time to taunt me about my appetite. Anyway I didn't hear you complaining earlier. You seemed downright grateful a couple of times," he pointed out complacently.

"Touché." It wasn't very gallant of him to remind her, but it was nothing less than the truth. He could make her wild, and make her love being that way. Laine giggled and gave him a playful sock in the ribs. "A director's chair, Murphy. How wicked of you."

He shook his head, grinning. "Before today, I'd have sworn that was impossible." He bit the fleshy pad of her thumb, then followed it up with a kiss. "You know, I've done some of my best work in that cupola. But I've never had so much fun doing it."

Laine's memory traveled further back, to the night in the tree house. "I'm getting to be an expert at climbing ladders to seduce you, Murphy."

"Sunshine, you can climb—"

"Never mind." She shut off his improper suggestion with her mouth. "I get the picture."

Laine sat up and tucked the white-piped navy sheet under her arms. She took her first clear look around the room. It was actually a suite that extended from the front of the house to the back. Both the huge bed, which was elevated, and an adjoining sitting area had expansive views of the ocean. With the windows open as they were now, the surf's lulling sound could be heard clearly. It was easy to see why Murphy loved being here. She was going to love it, too. But first she had to get everything out in the open.

"Are you ready now?" she asked gravely. "I've got to tell you sooner or later. If you'll just listen for a few minutes, I can get the past off my mind and we can talk about the future."

"Laine," he said, his lips touching her forehead. "I'm not insensitive. I know I cut you off before, but I had a reason. I wanted to show you that nothing's changed for me. I love you and want you with me. Whatever you have to say isn't going to make any difference in how I feel about that."

"I know, but it's important that I share this with you. I don't want us to start out with any secrets between us." She held his hand, not because she needed it for courage, but because she needed him. Period. And she could admit it without panicking. She'd come a long way since meeting Colin Murphy.

"Because Maureen and I were twins, I thought I always knew what she was thinking. How she'd react to any situation. I understood everything about her because she was the other half of me. Does that make sense?

Murphy nodded, but didn't speak. She felt his hand tighten on hers almost imperceptibly.

"It's ironic, but someone once jokingly dubbed us Sunshine and Shadow. You see, we really didn't act much like each other. I was always out with a crowd, having fun, while Maureen hid in her room, reading or studying. She truly thought people didn't like her, but that wasn't it at all. She was just incredibly shy and unsure of herself. Moving as often as we did only made the problem worse."

"But you were able to adjust, make new friends."

"Maureen used to say, 'It's so easy for you, Lainie.' It wasn't always, especially when I was younger. But I made myself do it. I guess I believed that if I acted like Sunshine, it would become a reality."

"I'd say that's pretty much how it turned out," Murphy said, fingering a strand of her hair.

Laine laughed soundlessly. "Maureen concentrated on becoming a brain and getting into medical school. It was as if she picked out one area in which to excel and threw her all into that. I doubt if she'd had half a dozen dates when she met Jeff. Nobody could believe the change in her. Oh, she still took her medical career seriously, but Jeff became the focus of her life. She adored him, doted on him, became quite obsessed by love."

"But he died," Murphy observed quietly.

Laine related the details about Jeff, her sister's withdrawal and eventual suicide. "At first I felt horrible guilt. I should have seen that her grief was beyond the norm. We were twins. I knew everything that went on inside her head, didn't I? Then I got angry. At Jeff's senseless death, but mostly at Maureen for choosing an equally senseless way of dealing with it."

"And somehow out of all that, you got scared of love. Afraid that if you let yourself become obsessed by a man as Maureen did with Jeff, then the same thing might happen to you."

"Architects aren't supposed to be perceptive about people," Laine said, surprised and a little unnerved.

"I'm not perceptive worth a damn about people. Just you." Murphy turned so that they were facing, and put his hands on her shoulders. "Don't you see, Laine, you were always more balanced than your sister. You were—are—interested in so many things it wears me out just thinking about it. And while I like the idea of you being just the tiniest bit obsessed with me, I can't see you ever letting that take control of your life. Not to the extent that you'd do anything like what Maureen did."

"That's the conclusion I reached when I analyzed why I was so terrified by what I claimed to want most. The rest was easy. And here I am. Ready to attain my goal."

"My God, I forgot about that! When's your birthday? Your deadline?"

Laine shrugged. "Afraid it came and went several days ago, the day of your brother's wedding, as a matter of fact."

"And you didn't mention it?" he demanded, as if her omission were a crime.

"It didn't seem appropriate at the time. By then, the prospect of meeting that deadline had me tied in knots."

"We've got to get a move on!" Murphy leaped from the bed. When she didn't spring up immediately, he gave her a smack on the bottom. "Shake it!"

"What on earth?" Laine protested. "I'm not going anywhere."

"Yes, you are. Right now." He was shouting over the noise of a running shower.

She wandered into the bathroom and peered into the glass shower enclosure. Murphy was soaping himself faster than she'd ever seen him do anything. "I'm not going anywhere," she repeated, "unless you give me a damned good reason."

He poked his head through a crack in the door. "We've got to get married, Sunshine. And fast."

"HAPPY BELATED BIRTHDAY, Elaine Randolph Murphy."

"Happy one-day anniversary, John Colin Murphy."

There was a faint ring of crystal touching as they toasted the two occasions. Laine met her husband's eyes, savored a small sip of the impressive French vintage and smiled dreamily. "No doubt about it. I'm a fallen woman. Led down the path of decadence by a fast-talking devil," she accused, pointing to a clock on the nightstand. "Almost noon and here we are. In bed again. Drinking champagne."

Murphy's grin indicated that he was no more concerned about her decline than she was. "We're on our honeymoon. Last night was our wedding night. We're supposed to do stuff like this." His free hand slid under her hair and curved around the back of her neck. Tugging gently, he brought her closer. "Come here, wife. Give me a good-morning kiss."

"I did that several hours ago. And a bunch of times since." Laine felt obliged to point out the reality of things. Beyond that, she didn't quibble about a minor technicality. She'd never had much resistance when it came to kissing Murphy. Now that he was her husband, the temptation was even greater.

When she had demonstrated the proper obedience, giving not one but several kisses, Murphy reclined lazily against a bank of pillows. He polished off his celebratory champagne and set the glass aside. "You know, I've always hated waking up. After all these years, I see that all I needed was an incentive."

Laine pretended to be offended. "So you're going to use sex in place of an alarm clock?"

Murphy looked at her strangely, as if he took her remark seriously. "Making love," he emphasized, "in the morning is nice. Different than at other times. Sort of fanciful and relaxed." He tipped up her chin with one finger. "But I meant that, knowing you'll be with me, I *want* to wake up. So I can hold you and talk to you. Tell you how much I love you."

Laine touched the corner of her eye. How embarrassing to go teary because her husband said he loved her. It wasn't as if he hadn't told her before. He said it often, and proved it in countless ways. "Oh, Murphy, I love you, too."

"Well, don't cry about it," he said gruffly. "I know I'm not the world's greatest bargain, not at all your idea of the perfect mate. But you're stuck with me." He hugged her tightly. "Cary Grant said it at the end of *Indiscreet*, remember? You'll like being married."

Laine laughed. "When I decided to come looking for you, I was afraid I might have to coerce you into marrying me. Instead I arrived to find you'd already bought the rings and made all the arrangements." She touched the wide gold band on Murphy's left hand. It was identical to her own. "Talk about shotgun weddings."

"I didn't want to take any chances once I got hold of you again." Murphy's tone turned very somber, his eyes serious. "Laine, I'll work real hard at being a good husband, and I promise I'll do better at it than you think."

She looked deeply into his eyes, accepting and reassuring. "You're just right as you are. I set up all those silly requirements because I didn't know what I wanted, or needed. Lucky for me that I ran into you when I did." Laine kissed his chest, his shoulder, his chin. "Murphy, thank you for not giving up on me. And for allowing me time to resolve everything in my mind."

He placed her hand on his heart. "It wasn't easy to let you go. I was so positive we were right for each other that I just wanted to grab you and hang on. I was like a snarling bear after you left. My family couldn't wait to get rid of me. I had to promise not to open my mouth before Josh would drive me back to Savannah where I'd left my car." He laughed as he recalled his crankiness. "Josh also told me not to come back unless I brought you."

Laine pulled away and crossed her arms. "Then it's a good thing I'm here, isn't it? Otherwise, you'd never get to return to your tree house. Come to think of it," she said with a gleam in her eyes, "I wouldn't mind going back there myself. Fond memories, and all that."

Murphy reached for her with a matching gleam. "Forget return engagements. We have a whole bunch of places here that need to be christened first. There's a terrific little cove on the south end of the island. Let's go there at midnight and I'll . . ."

"I DIDN'T THINK you'd really do that in the cove at midnight, Murphy. You're shameless." Surf foamed quietly around their ankles as they walked along the beach toward the house. Laine was wrapped in an oversize beach towel; her fingers were intertwined with Murphy's.

He stopped and spread his arms wide. "A strong argument in favor of having your own island, no matter how small."

His towel wasn't as modestly deployed as Laine's. Getting used to living with a totally uninhibited man was going to be interesting, she could see. But Murphy, quirks and all, was worth a few adjustments.

"Murphy, I know how important this island is to you. And I can see why. I honestly don't want you to give it up for me." Earlier that day, he'd told her he was prepared to return to Atlanta with her the next week.

"I'm not giving it up for you, Sunshine. I'm going to share it with you. Just as you'll share your home with me. It's only a matter of being practical. You can't work from here. I can work in Atlanta."

"That's sweet of you, but—"

"This will be our special retreat. We'll come as often as we can, just the two of us."

"Murphy, don't you think you're getting carried away? You only just got married, a radical enough change in your life-style. Now you're talking about moving back to the city. Isn't all that a bit much?"

"Sunshine, you've rearranged your thinking to make me a part of your life. I want to do the same for you. Hear that? I *want* to. Besides, haven't you learned that it's useless to argue with Murphy's law?"

Laine thought back to the first time they met, and his personal definition of that law. What I want, I take. "You wanted me," she whispered.

"And I've got you. Forever."

Laine had never imagined that she could be this happy. Overcome with love, she stood on tiptoe and feathered a kiss onto her husband's mouth. "Aren't I incredibly lucky that we wanted exactly the same thing?"

Epilogue

"RIGHT THERE IS WHERE we'll build your tree house, son."

One-year-old John Randolph Murphy regarded his father out of solemn golden eyes before he, too, pointed at the thick clump of pines near the back edge of their property. "My house."

"That's right. As soon as you're a little older, I'll help you build it, but it will be yours. Off limits to everyone else. A man needs his privacy."

Murphy chuckled and the little boy in his arms squirmed, then echoed the laugh, man-to-man. "Don't tell her I told you this, but if you're very lucky, someday a beautiful woman will come here and seduce you. Like your mother did me."

"Mom," John announced with a nod of his head. "Sunshine."

Smiling proudly, Murphy sat on a stump beneath a flowering pink dogwood tree and bounced his son on his knee in a mock horseback ride. "At the time she wasn't sure enough to tell me she loved me. But she must have known it in her heart, because she took a big risk that night."

Laine stepped into the clearing just as he opened his mouth to continue. "Don't you dare tell him that he was conceived in your tree house a week before we were married, Murphy."

He laughed and lifted John to his mother's outstretched arms. "Why not? This morning, before the birthday party, Smokin' Joe actually teased me about rushing things."

"I didn't think The General had it in him to tease about anything. But it's amazing to watch him playing grandfather. He's positively mellowed. He assured me that John is a born pilot. Only one year old today, and already showing he's got the right stuff," Laine said, with a rueful smile. In the year since their son's birth, Laine's parents had found any number of excuses to visit Atlanta. Now they were talking about retiring there and having Murphy design them a house.

Smokin' Joe wasn't the only one who had changed. One of the first things Murphy had done when they'd come back to Atlanta after their wedding was to buy these two acres of wooded land on a hill north of the Perimeter. Then he had devoted all his time to getting their new home finished by Christmas. Less than three months later, they were parents.

Before Laine had even suspected that she was pregnant, Murphy had suggested they not wait too long before starting their family. After all, he'd reasoned, they weren't getting any younger. And if they intended to have more than one, they shouldn't waste much time.

Being married to Colin Murphy was everything—and more—than Laine had hoped for.

"I guess we'd better be getting back before they send the troops out to find us," she said, dropping a kiss on her son's cheek and hugging him tightly. "Your parents and Claire and Ted need to get on the road. Then I have some last minute packing to do before we leave."

Murphy draped his arm around her shoulders as they started for the house. "Don't worry, Sunshine. They'll take good care of him."

"I'm being silly. He's going to have a great time being spoiled by his grandparents. I guess it's just because we've never left him overnight before."

"Bet I know a way to distract you." He whispered his plans for their second honeymoon on the island. He ignored Laine's scolding to ask, "How about it, John? Don't you think it's about time we started working on a sister for you?"

"A pony," the little boy replied distinctly. "Smokin' Joe says I need a pony."

Laine and Murphy exchanged shocked looks, both at the complete sentence and at the nickname for his grandfather. She gave him an I-told-you-so glare and said, "Now will you please pay attention when I tell you to watch what you say? Otherwise the whole world will know our secrets."

He grinned at Laine and then at his son. "John Randolph Murphy, I love your mother. And I want the whole world to know it."

Step into a world of pulsing adventure, gripping emotion and lush sensuality with these evocative love stories penned by today's best-selling authors in the highest romantic tradition. Pursuing their passionate dreams against a backdrop of the past's most colorful and dramatic moments, our vibrant heroines and dashing heroes will make history come alive for you.

Watch for two new Harlequin Historicals each month, available wherever Harlequin books are sold. History was never so much fun—you won't want to miss a single moment!

Harlequin Superromance

**Here are the longer, more involving stories you
have been waiting for... Superromance.**

Modern, believable novels of love, full of the complex
joys and heartaches of real people.

Intriguing conflicts based on today's constantly
changing life-styles.

Four new titles every month.
Available wherever paperbacks are sold.

SUPER-1

TEARS IN THE RAIN

STARRING
CHRISTOPHER CAVZENOVE AND
SHARON STONE

BASED ON A NOVEL BY
PAMELA WALLACE

PREMIERING IN NOVEMBER

Harlequin Temptation dares to be different!

Once in a while, we Temptation editors spot a romance that's truly innovative. To make sure *you* don't miss any one of these outstanding selections, we'll mark them for you.

EDITOR'S CHOICE

When the "Editors' Choice" fold-back appears on a Temptation cover, you'll know we've found that extra-special page-turner!

THE

Temptation

EDITORS

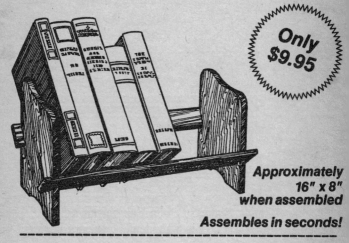